ARGY

FOLK TALES

ARGYLL FOLK TALES

BOB PEGG

To the memory of Roy Palmer,
for his good company and encouragement

First published 2015

The History Press
The Mill, Brimscombe Port
Stroud, Gloucestershire, GL5 2QG
www.thehistorypress.co.uk

British Library Cataloguing in Publication Data.
A catalogue record for this book is available from the British Library.

ISBN 978 0 7524 9215 5

Typesetting and origination by The History Press
Printed in Great Britain

Contents

Acknowledgements

Thanks to Mike Anderson, Rachel Butter, Brigadier Iain MacFarlane, and Bill Taylor, who all gave advice and enlightenment on various topics.

Thanks to Kilmartin House Museum for the Sounding Dunadd project, which gave me the opportunity to research and tell some of the stories that appear in *Argyll Folk Tales*.

Thanks to the Enterprise Music Scotland Traditional Arts Small Grants Fund, for financial help in visiting places mentioned in these stories.

Access to the private library of the late Dugald MacArthur was enormously helpful in putting this book together.

Particular thanks go to Mairi MacArthur: for help with matters of Gaelic, for sharing her knowledge of Argyll and particularly of Mull and Iona, for research in the Library of the Gaelic Society of Inverness and elsewhere, for reading and commenting on the contents of *Argyll Folk Tales* at various stages in its writing, and for many great meals which helped keep a smile on my face.

All illustrations are by the author.

INTRODUCTION

To begin with a legend.

On a stormy day in 1572 a funeral barge was towing a stone coffin across Loch Etive, heading for Ardchattan Priory on the west bank of the loch. The coffin was huge. It had been made to accommodate the mortal remains of a seven foot-tall man, Bishop John Carswell, known as a' Chorra-ghritheach – the Heron – because of his long legs and the bird-like hunch in which he held his shoulders.

In the turmoil of the crossing, the rope securing the vessel bearing the coffin broke, and the bishop drifted away into the teeth of the storm. The coffin was found several days later, washed up close to the priory, at a place which is still called Rubha Charsalaich – Carswell's Point.

Carswell, who was born in 1522, lived in Carnasserie Castle in Kilmartin Glen, close to the coast at a midway point in mainland Argyll. At a time of great religious and civil unrest, he was the first Protestant Bishop of the Isles, and is remembered primarily for his translation into Gaelic of John Knox's *Book of Common Order*, which, in 1567, was the first book to be printed in the Gaelic language.

In his Dedication to the Earl of Argyll, Carswell railed against a contemporary world where people were happy to pay to listen to Gaelic songs and verse inspired by 'vain, hurtful, earthly, lying stories' of legendary characters, who included 'Fionn mac Cumhail and his giants'. His lament confirms the widespread popularity in the Gaelic Highlands of a literature that drew on old Irish legends.

Written and oral sources dating from *The Book of the Dean of Lismore*, compiled in manuscript in the first half of the sixteenth century, to the publication of James Macpherson's controversial *Ossian* in 1760, and right up to tales told today, are evidence of how widely the exploits of Finn MacCool and other ancient worthies have been celebrated in verse, song and story.

Finn MacCool is a character in a handful of the fireside tales included in this book. The latter part of the nineteenth century, when many of the stories included here were taken down, was a time of great enthusiasm for the collecting of old stories, songs and music, not just in Scotland, but right across Europe. The Grimm brothers' collection of German folk tales, *Children's and Household Tales*, first published in 1812, had become an international bestseller, and there was a widespread conviction that if old lore wasn't recorded it would vanish within a couple of generations.

Argyll Folk Tales owes a huge debt to story collectors from this period – their names and works appear in the select bibliography at the end of the book – but an inspiration for them all was John Francis Campbell.

J.F. Campbell, born in 1821, was sole heir to the island of Islay. When he was a boy he was delivered into the care of the family's piper, another John Campbell:

> ... from him I learned to be hardy and healthy and I learned Gaelic; I learned to swim and to take care of myself, and to talk to everybody who chose to talk to me ... Thus I made early acquaintance with a blind fiddler who could recite stories.

With such an upbringing Campbell would surely have made an enlightened laird, but in 1847, because of debt, his father was forced to sell Islay. Nevertheless, Iain Òg Ìle – Young John of Islay – went on to make his way in the world with great success, as a courtier, civil servant, and inveterate traveller, excelling as a linguist, scientist and folklorist.

J.F. Campbell's enthusiasm for what he called 'storyology' was encouraged by his friend Sir George Webb Dasent, and by the publication in 1859 of Dasent's *Popular Tales from the Norse*. Though Campbell himself was in London at the time, immersed in the preparation of the Report of the Lighthouse Commission, he contacted Hector MacLean, his old tutor who was now a headmaster on Islay, asking him to take time off to begin the collecting of Gaelic folk tales in the islands. Hector Urquhart, a gamekeeper at Ardkinglas on the mainland, and John Dewar, who was a woodcutter on the Inveraray estates, were added to the team, and in record time *Popular Tales of the West Highlands* appeared in four volumes, between 1860 and 1862. Most of the stories are presented bilingually, in Gaelic with a literal translation into English, together with Campbell's own extensive notes which still make lively and provocative reading.

The endeavours of Campbell and his companions brought together a collection of nearly 800 tales, many of which remain to be published. The range of material is vast, from old Fingalian lays to the long, magical quest stories that folklorists call *märchen*. The tales were taken down scrupulously by hand, sometimes over the course of several days, and Campbell's insistence on presenting them unaltered, together with information about who told them, is still a touchstone for folklorists.

Argyll is an area whose waters are as significant as its land mass, with freshwater lochs, fjords and the sea itself, along with islands – Mull, Islay, Jura, Iona and more – which are self-contained worlds. At one time its accepted boundaries extended from the Mull of Kintyre in the south to Cape Wrath in the far north-west, but the stories here, with a little leeway, come from within the current administrative area, from the southern tip of Kintyre almost as far as Fort William in the north, east to the Firth of Clyde and Rannoch Moor, and including most of the Inner Isles.

The history of Argyll is rich and varied. There's strong evidence that 13,000 years ago, among the frozen terrain of the last Ice Age, itinerant hunters were sheltering in caves in what, today, is the Kilmelford area. Some 7,300 years after this, people from settled farming communities began to house their dead in the chambered cairns of Kilmartin Glen.

Starting around 2,800 years ago, the construction of lake dwellings called crannogs, fortified towers known as brochs, and hilltop forts, is evidence of a land-owning elite which probably needed to keep an eye both on near neighbours and on threats from further afield. One of these forts, Dunadd at the south end of Kilmartin Glen, became the hub of the Kingdom of Dál Riata, whose people had close links to Ulster, and which lasted in relative stability until its end in 839, when the area came under Viking domination. The result was a chaotic grouping of warlords engaged in power struggles and shifting alliances; and out of this emerged the Kingship of the Isles, which was established by the Celto-Norse ruler Somerled around 1150, and which led in turn to the Lordship of the Isles, an alliance centred on Islay which lasted until 1493.

The clan system which had been developing for several hundred years now dominated the Highlands. A social structure where the power and status of a relatively small number of extended families depended primarily on the possession of lands, naturally led to a period in which feuds and attendant violence were rife, extending outwards into religious and civil wars until the middle of the eighteenth century. Ordinary people lived at the mercy of these upheavals. They were essentially a peasantry, afforded protection and subsistence on the land, in return for rent in kind and an obligation to fight for their chieftain when commanded.

During the century prior to the time John Francis Campbell and his companions began collecting stories, Argyll had undergone immense changes. The 5th Duke of Argyll was an agricultural improver and innovator who, from 1770 to1806, gradually reorganised his extensive estates into individual smallholdings or crofts. The years after his death, however, brought further disruption, when many tenants found themselves displaced to make way for big, and more profitable, sheep farms. The construction of a proper road network, and the opening of the Crinan Canal in 1801, improved communications immeasurably. A steamer service from Glasgow that began in 1819 opened up island and coastal communities to a new wave of visitors. James Johnson, writing in

1832, describes an Oban which had previously been a small village with a single inn:

> On two days of the week and at certain hours of the day, three steamers and a stage coach are seen approaching ... from the four points of the compass ...
>
> The whole of Oban is instantly aroused from torpor to fervid excitement. The innkeepers are on the alert, while the scouts, vid-ettes [small boats] and purveyors of the rival hotels are on active service and full pay ...
>
> Meanwhile, the contents of the steamers – men, women, children, sheep, poultry, pigs, dogs, salmon, herrings, cakes, trunks, bags, baskets, hampers, books, portfolios, maps, guns, fishing tackle and thousands of other articles are in rapid transit from vessel to vessel – from steamer to coach to steamer ...

Later, for the ten years following 1846, a potato blight caused many people great hardship, and the population of Argyll, which had already been declining, started to diminish dramatically. People were leaving either for the Lowlands – primarily the Glasgow area – or for new worlds across the sea where earlier waves of kin were already making good lives for themselves.

A constant among all this change was popular entertainment, which included storytelling. Stories were enjoyed by people of all ages – adults as much as children – and the storytellers came from many different walks of life. Contributors to *Popular Tales of the West Highlands* included ministers' and farmers' wives, ministers themselves, servants, a fisherman, a roadman, a woodcutter, a blind fiddler, and a 'travelling tinker'. Storytellers themselves could draw on a vast international repertoire of tales which had slipped and slithered between different cultures and languages, in some cases for thousands of years, constantly accommodating themselves to the times and places in which they landed.

The themes and scenarios of the stories are universal, and range from magic-infused fantasy, through heroic adventure and love in adversity, to demonic encounters and black farce. Like all popular entertainment they offer comfort and reassurance: clueless lads somehow manage to overcome all obstacles; young women win a man through resourcefulness; giants are defeated, and curses lifted. But the stories also have a darker side which reflects the fears of the people who told them, speaking of sudden death, magical forces that are hard or impossible to combat, and mysterious childhood ailments which can only be explained as the effects of malign supernatural forces.

One of the most charming and disarming aspects of folk tales is the way they adapt to take on details from the everyday lives of the individual storytellers. The oatmeal bannock, a staple food for centuries in the Highlands, has an important role in a number of stories here. The king lives in a house, rather than a palace, and that house, with its servants, resembles the minister's manse or the laird's mansion. At a time when it was common for young women to travel, either to do seasonal work or to go into service, the kist in the Argyll version of the Cinderella story – 'The King Who Wished to Marry His Daughter' – is, as J.F. Campbell observed, the chest:

> ... which every well provided highland lass takes to service. Such kists, and such lassies seated on them may be seen in every highland steam-boat ...
>
> The contents of all are alike; the clothes of generations. The mother's Sunday dresses, and the grandmother's, with some fine shawl, or cap, or bonnet ...

So the Argyll stories are both universal and very much of Argyll itself. Many of them are attached to particular places, and the tales could be recalled, or even read, when visiting those places, while the reader far from Argyll can recreate the characters, scenarios and landscapes in his or her imagination. I have greatly enjoyed retelling these tales, and discovering anew their drama, pathos and humour. However and wherever you read them, I hope you will enjoy them too. Please think about passing them on in the way they've been handed down for so many years – by telling them aloud, in your own words.

A Note on the Text

The majority of the stories in this collection were originally taken down in Gaelic more than a hundred years ago, and then translated into English by the collectors or their contemporaries. I've based my retellings on these translations, in almost every instance keeping to the structure and broad details of the original story. But the foremost aim has been to produce what I hope are lively and entertaining tales for non-specialist readers. While writing, my head has echoed with the voices of some of the Scottish storytellers it's been my privilege to know and hear in performance. Among them are Alec Williamson and Essie Stewart, both representatives of the Highland Traveller tradition, Stanley Robertson of Aberdeen, Sheila Stewart of Rattray, Orkney's Tom Muir, and Lawrence Tulloch from Shetland. For this book, the most insistent voice has been that of Duncan Williamson. Duncan was born into a Traveller family in 1928, in a woodland clearing by the shores of Loch Fyne in Argyll. He became Scotland's best-known storyteller, entertaining audiences around the world until his death in 2007. The stories in *Argyll Folk Tales* mirror the vast range of his repertoire, from the epics of questing adventure, through mysterious encounters with the supernatural, to broad, unbuttoned humour.

Notes on individual stories are given at the beginning of each chapter, and occasionally at the beginning of a story itself. For readers who would like to dig deeper into these Argyll tales, there is a select bibliography at the end of the book. Many of the older key works are available online – a particularly useful site is www.archive.org.

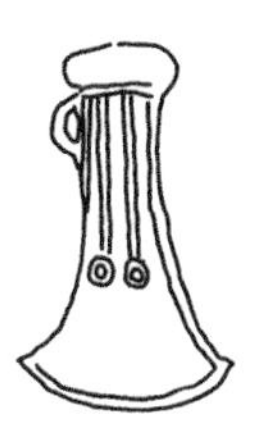

Not Long After the Beginning

We can only imagine where and how the first stories were told, and in what forgotten language. Many folk tales have long pedigrees. The story of Deirdre – included in 'On the Run' – exists in a manuscript version from the eleventh century; and an episode in 'Conall Yellow Claw' in 'Tellers of Tales' is close enough to be a re-telling of the encounter with Polyphemus the Cyclops in Homer's *Odyssey*, an episode which appears in a play by Euripides that was performed around 2,400 years ago.

The four tales in this first chapter hint at the kinds of story that could have been told in prehistoric times.

The dramatic life and death of the gigantic Cailleach Bheur are played out in a landscape where legend crosses over into myth. Her story hints at religious beliefs that could have been held in north Britain before Christianity took hold.

'The Song of the Wind' is an adaptation of two Native American stories, dedicated to the early hunting peoples. The grouping of stars in the tale of the Magic Monster Bear is the constellation we call the Plough, which itself is part of the larger constellation, the Great Bear.

Like many of the stories in *Argyll Folk Tales*, 'The Two Brothers' has travel by sea as one of its central themes. It takes place in a time when a voyage to a neighbouring island was an adventure as unpredictable and hazardous as a journey to a planet in a distant galaxy might be today.

The story of Cinderella, in its many different versions, is widespread throughout the world. While it might not go back as far as the Ice Age – a suggestion which has been made – a Chinese version was written down as long ago as the middle of the ninth century. The Argyll Cinderella story, 'The King Who Wished to Marry His Daughter', is richer and stranger than the eighteenth-century Perrault version on which popular pantomimes, animations and films have been based. As with the story of 'The Two Brothers', there is a sea voyage, but in an unusual vessel.

– The Cailleach Bheur –

The Cailleach Bheur – the Old Thundering Woman – was born, if that's how she came into being, in the times when there were forests where there are now seas. Her fame was widespread. The Revd Charles Stewart, who contributed the 1792 entry for Strachur and Stralachlan to *The Statistical Account of Scotland*, wrote of a very large stone which was dedicated to her. The stone stood on a high ridge:

> … which separates Stralachlan from Glendaruel. There is a descent from it on every side. The prospect from it is very extensive. It is called *Cailleach-vear* or *vera*. In the dark ages of superstition, it was personified, and said to have a considerable property in cattle. *Cailleach-vear* makes a conspicuous figure in the marvellous tales of the country people, over a great part of the West Highlands. Her residence was said to be on the highest mountains; that she could step with ease, and in a moment, from one district to another; when offended, that she caused the flood, which destroyed the corns, and laid the low grounds under water …

This gigantic woman ranged far and wide in her travels. One story says that she came originally from Norway – perhaps she was related to the Norse Giants – carrying a pannier full of rocks and earth on her shoulder. She was heading for the Scottish mainland when the strap of the pannier broke, and the contents tumbled out into the ocean, creating the Western Isles; while Ailsa Craig – the beacon rock in the Firth of Clyde – dropped through a hole in her apron. The Cailleach used to drive her goats across the rocks at the falls of Connel – her stepping stones – and she had her cheese-vats close by at Benderloch. Her horse left its hoof print on a rock on Ben Cruachan, and on the slopes of the same mountain she kept her cow, walking every morning from the Mull of Kintyre to give it water. The well was a magic one. It was covered by a massive granite slab which should only be lifted between sunrise and sunset. One warm, sunny day, after watering her cow, the Cailleach fell asleep and, when the sun set, the well was still open. Water poured out, and rushed down the slopes of Ben Cruachan to fill the glen below, and that's how Loch Awe came into being.

However extensive her journeyings, the Cailleach Bheur had her home on the island of Mull; she would milk her sheep and goats at Cailleach Point, on the north of the island, and when she sneezed the explosion could be heard as far away as Coll. Her herds of deer were nurtured off to the west, in the waters between the Dhu Heartach skerry and the Torran Rocks. And it was on Mull that the Cailleach's long life came to an end. Once every hundred years she

would bathe in Loch Bà, in the middle of the island. She entered the waters as a withered old hag, and came out of the loch revitalised, a beautiful young woman. The immersion had to take place very early in the day, before any of the birds or animals were awake; but on this particular morning, as the Cailleach was thundering down the slopes to the loch side, away in the distance a sheepdog barked. She stopped and cocked her head to one side. The dog barked again, and the Cailleach tottered and fell. She died there, within inches of the water.

~ The Song of the Wind ~

This happened long before the farming people put up the big stones and built the cairn tombs in Kilmartin Glen – and long before anyone had called the place by that name. In those days the land that wasn't saturated with water was covered over with forest. The first people came along the coast in boats made from wicker frames covered in hide. They made shelters in the caves at the edge of the sea, and they fished, ate the plants and berries that flourished in the forests, and hunted the animals which had drifted in as the ice sheet shrank northwards. At first they travelled around, never staying in one place for very long, following the bounties of fish, flesh and plant life that the successive seasons brought; but after a while they began to use axes with sharp flint heads to cut down the forest trees – oak, pine and hazel – and to make clearings where they could build huts. These villages became bases to return to after hunting, fishing and foraging expeditions. The people who lived in them felt more secure than when they had been constantly on the move, and they began to name themselves after animals that had qualities they admired.

Most of the tribes got on well enough with their neighbours, and at particular times of the year they would join together to feast, sing and dance. It was at one of these celebrations that a boy from the Wolf people fell in love with the daughter of the chief of the Swan people. At earlier feasts he'd hardly noticed her, just one of a group of girls who hung around braiding each others' hair, dancing

together and giggling a lot. Now, suddenly, she seemed to be the most beautiful creature he had ever seen. During the dancing he had managed to get quite close to her, but she had looked past him, into the smoke of the fire, and he imagined that she was dreaming of marrying the son of a chief.

When there was a break in the dancing, the old storyteller sat by the edge of the fire, and began the tale of the Magic Monster Bear:

In this family there were three hunters, and they were famous for never giving up on their prey. Once they were on the trail, they would hunt to the final kill. They had a dog called Four Eyes, whose eyes had black circles round them. Four Eyes was able to see tracks that were invisible to humans.

A message reached the hunters that a nearby village was being menaced by a massive bear. The children no longer played out in the woods, houses were barred, and when the villagers woke in the morning they found giant paw prints in the earth around their homes.

The hunters set off through the woods, with Four Eyes running beside them. They were determined to help the people of the threatened village.

As they got closer to the village, they noticed that there was no sign of any animals among the trees, and no bird song.

They came to an old pine tree. High up on its trunk were gashes where a great beast had stood on its hind legs and ripped into the bark with its claws. The first hunter tried to touch the claw marks with the tip of his spear, but he couldn't reach. 'This isn't an ordinary bear,' he said. 'This is the Magic Monster Bear.'

'If that's true,' said the second hunter, 'it could be good for us. I've never seen the Magic Monster Bear myself, but I've spoken to old people who have. They say that the Magic Monster Bear is a treacherous creature; he can creep up on you and eat you without you even realising that he's there. But, once you've spotted his tracks, he's forced to flee.'

The third hunter said, 'I hope we've brought plenty of food. It sounds like this is going to be a long hunt.'

The hunters arrived at the village. It was a sad-looking place. In the very centre, where a fire once burned day and night, there was a pile of grey ash. The doors of the huts were barred, and there was no sign of the women, the children and the old people. The men kept guard; with clubs and spears in their hands, they eyed the fringes of the forest.

The head man came forward to speak to the hunters. Yes, he said, there was certainly a bear. Even though none of the villagers had seen it yet, every morning, when they woke, they found giant paw prints in the earth around their huts, and when they looked up they saw that the trees were scarred with huge claw marks. They were preparing for the day when the bear would come out of the forest in broad daylight.

'We don't think this is an ordinary bear,' said the first hunter. 'We think it's the Magic Monster Bear. But don't worry, we'll track it down and kill it. We never give up on our prey.'

'We've got Four Eyes the dog,' said the second hunter. 'He can see tracks that are invisible to humans.'

'Do you have any food, and somewhere we could lie down and rest before we start the hunt? And maybe a couple of pretty girls to keep us company?' said the third hunter.

'He's just joking,' said the first hunter. And they set off to find the bear.

They hunted for days, and there was no sign of any bear, though all the time they had the feeling that they were being watched from within the woods. The third hunter had brought along some food, some deer meat and fat, pounded together with berries, which he was keeping in a pouch. When he emptied the contents of the pouch into his hand, white, wriggling worms slid out. The Magic Monster Bear had put a spell on the food. But the third hunter was so hungry that he ate the worms anyway.

As the hunt continued, the air became colder. At the end of a long day, when the three hunters were beginning to lose hope of ever finding the bear, Four Eyes yelped. He'd spotted tracks. Immediately the bear appeared close by, with its long sharp claws, its long sharp teeth, and its burning red eyes. It was running away from the hunters. Its fur was white. It looked like a ghost.

Four Eyes kept close to the bear, snapping at its heels, and the hunters followed as best they could. After a while the third hunter got fed-up with running. He faked a fall and pretended to twist his ankle so the other two had to pick him up and carry him and his spear. It was hard for them to keep going with the extra weight, and the bear was pulling ahead, up the mountain slopes. Then it turned and looked down at Four Eyes. It reared up on its hind legs, opened its mouth, and bared its long sharp teeth.

'I'm fine now,' said the third hunter. 'Let me down.' As soon as he was back on his feet he grabbed his spear, let out a yell, and ran off after the bear. The bear turned and took the mountain slope, with Four Eyes and the third hunter close behind.

The other two hunters watched them disappear into the clouds at the top of the mountain. They were exhausted with carrying their companion, but they kept on the trail, climbing higher and higher until it grew dark and they could no longer see the ground beneath their feet. Eventually, in the distance, they saw a light and, when they got closer, there was the third hunter. He had already killed and butchered the bear. Its meat was turning on a spit over a fire, and the white fat dripped down, sizzling on the embers.

'Hey boys, where have you been?' he said. 'Come and sit down. Eat some of the bear meat I've killed and cooked for you.'

When the feast was over, even the third hunter was more than full.

'Look,' said the first hunter, pointing downwards. There was no sign of the mountain. All around them were glittering points of light. They hadn't noticed that the bear had run right up off the top of the mountain and high into the sky. They were sitting among the stars.

'Look there,' said the second hunter. The bear's bones were slowly coming together; muscle and sinew, flesh and fur formed on them. The bear stood up and lumbered away.

'Come on!' shouted the third hunter. He grabbed his spear and set off in pursuit, followed by Four Eyes and the other two hunters.

And the hunters are still up there in the sky, chasing the Magic Monster Bear. There are four stars that make the body of the bear, and following the bear are three more stars – the hunters. And if you look closely and you have really sharp eyes, you can see that the middle hunter is actually two stars. One of them is Four Eyes the dog.

As the year begins to grow old, and the hunt crosses the sky, the bear turns upside down, and people say, 'The lazy hunter has killed the bear.' The bear's blood drips down on to the trees and turns the leaves red. Then the dripping fat falls on the grass and turns it white.

When spring comes round the bear turns over, its bones come together, and it starts to run, and the hunt continues until the following autumn, when the feast begins again.

After the boy heard the story of the Magic Monster Bear, it was plain to him what he should do. Early the next morning he took his spear and his bow and arrows, and a pouch with deer meat in, and set off into the forest. He planned to kill an animal, something big like the bear in the story, take it to the chief's daughter and throw it down on to the ground in front of her. 'Now,' he would say, 'see what I've caught and killed just for you. Don't you think

I'm a fine hunter?' The chief's daughter would fall in love with him and a marriage would soon take place.

The boy hunted all day, going deeper and deeper into the forest, and further and further away from the huts of the Wolf people. He heard rustlings in the undergrowth and saw distant shapes that might have been large animals, but as the sun began to set and the forest shadows lengthened he knew that he was going to catch nothing, and that he would have to spend the night there, because he was too far from home to find his way back safely in the darkness. He climbed high up into the branches of a tree, making sure that he wasn't sharing it with a lynx. He shook the food, a ball of venison, fat and berries, out of his pouch and ate it, listening to the wolves howling in the distance. Then he closed his eyes and went to sleep.

While he slept, the boy had a dream. The first thing he dreamed was a sound like nothing he had heard before; it was as if the wind was singing. In the dream it was first light. He climbed to the bottom of the tree and saw that there was a path leading deeper into the forest. He followed the path until it opened out into a clearing. In the middle of the clearing was a massive pine tree, and sitting on an old hollow branch of the tree was an eagle, which was pecking holes in the branch. A wind blew through the clearing into the hollow branch, and out of the holes that the eagle had pecked, and that was how the beautiful sound was made.

In the morning the boy woke and climbed down the tree, and there was a path, just like the one in his dream. He followed the path into the heart of the forest until he came to a clearing. In the middle of the clearing was a massive pine tree. The boy broke an old, hollow branch from the tree and took it back to the clearing where the Wolf people had their huts. He spent all day making sure the branch was completely hollow, and cutting holes in it with his flint knife, in the same places that the dream eagle had pecked. Somehow he knew where to carve a notch in the end of the branch, so that when he blew down it, it whistled; and somehow he knew that if he put his fingers on the holes and lifted them up and put them down again while he blew, the branch would make a sound like the wind singing.

When evening came, the boy took his singing branch and went through the forest until he came to the edge of the clearing where the Swan people had their huts. He stood there, among the shadows, put the end of the branch to his lips and blew. The sound of the wind singing drifted across the clearing until it came to the hut that the chief's daughter shared with her family. She was ready to go to sleep, but when she heard the beautiful sound she had to find out where it was coming from. She crept out of the hut and walked through the darkness until she came face to face with the boy, who was playing just for her. And – the story says – when she looked into his eyes she fell instantly in love with him.

Not long after that, there was a great feast, and the boy from the Wolf tribe was married to the daughter of the chief of the Swan people. When the old chief, the girl's father, died, the young man became chief in his place. He did well enough, but he knew there was something else he could do better, so one day he handed over the job to one of his wife's brothers, and set out into the woods to collect old, hollow branches from the trees. Each one he turned into a wind singer, and each had its own particular song – and so he became the first flute maker. Word of his talents spread, and people travelled for long distances, sometimes hundreds of miles, to trade for his flutes. They brought finely woven cloth, stone axe heads, jet beads that he in turn could exchange for food and clothing for his family. The flutes became so popular that the flute-maker trained his whole family to make the instruments. Flutes were made and were taken away by their proud new owners, but there was one flute he would never part with. It was the very first wind singer, the instrument inspired by the eagle that pecked holes in the hollow branch of a massive pine tree. Every evening, after the making was finished, the man who had fallen in love with the chief's daughter, all those years before, would take out that first flute and play for his wife and children, and later for his grandchildren and their children too. And when he'd taken his very last breath, the flute was placed in his hands, a companion to go with him to the next world.

~ THE TWO BROTHERS ~

A very long time ago, there was hardly anybody living on the island of Mull, just a handful of families on the south coast of what's now called the Ross, where the settlement of Carsaig is today. No one knows when and how their ancestors arrived there, but these were people who stuck to the land. They had no idea what sailing was. They thought the little islets they could see from the coast were other worlds.

One day they noticed a strange thing coming towards them from the sea. At a distance they thought it was a horse with a tree growing out of its back, but as it neared the shore they saw something equally mystifying – a huge wicker basket covered in hides, floating in on the tide. In the basket was a man. He had a supply of fresh water with him, and some hazelnuts. The people named him Hidebasket.

Hidebasket had come over from the mainland coast, looking for adventure. When he tried to explain this to the Mull people they began to understand that there were other communities apart from their own little world. They liked Hidebasket, and made him welcome, and he stayed with them a good while. He helped them improve their way of living and taught them new skills. It's said that the first cheese on Mull was made when Hidebasket showed the Mull people the trick of putting marsh marigold stalks into milk, to produce curds and whey.

After a year another boat appeared off the coast. Like the first, it had one man in it, and it was covered with skins. The man had come looking for Hidebasket, who was his brother. The Mull people named him Skinman, and they got on as well with him as they did with Hidebasket. The brothers saw that there were a lot of trees close to the shore, so they set to, to make a big boat. When the boat was built, they christened her *Six Oars*. The brothers made *Six Oars* seaworthy, and set off with a crew to explore the uncharted ocean. They came first to the island of Jura, but the natives were scared by the sight of the boat and wouldn't let them ashore, driving them away with stones. When they reached

Colonsay, the people there tried to throw sand in their eyes, so they moved on to Islay. The shore was deserted, so the brothers and their crew hauled *Six Oars* up on to the beach and set off inland to see if they could find any sign of people or a house. At night-fall they met an old man, who was keeping an eye on his cattle. He thought the strangers must be from another part of the island, as no one had been known to leave, or to come there from else-where. When Hidebasket spoke to him, the old man said he had an odd accent for an Islay man.

'I'm not from the island,' said Hidebasket.

'In that case, where are you from, and what do you want?'

'I'm here to ask for help, and to give what I can in return.'

The old man made a fire, and the sailors sat with him until dawn, and in the first light they saw that there were houses and people. The locals were very friendly, and the voyagers stayed on for a year and showed them how to build boats. Hidebasket found the time to fall in love. He got married to a local girl, and she went with him when he, Skinman and their crew decided at last to return to Mull.

Six Oars wasn't long at sea when she became enveloped in a thick, dark fog. There was no way of knowing where land might be, so they drifted for ages until the boat came to rest by an unknown shore. They heard the sound of heavy footsteps crushing the shells and shingle, and a huge man came out of the mist. He grabbed the prow of the boat and hauled *Six Oars* up on to the beach with the crew still in her. The big man invited them back to his house, and made them welcome.

Hidebasket asked the big man's daughter if he and his compan-ions might get something to drink. She brought in a two-hooped wooden dish full of milk, put it down on the floor, and went out of the room. One of the party tried to lift the dish, but he wasn't able. Three of them tried, and still it couldn't be raised. The girl came back. 'For all your thirst,' she said, 'it doesn't look as if you've touched the milk.'

'We couldn't lift the dish,' said Hidebasket, 'and we're not used to bowing down like cattle to drink.'

The girl picked the dish up by one of its ears. She held it out for them, and asked where they were from. They told her they had come from the Indigo Isle, and were headed for the Isle of Mountains.

'That must be Mull,' said the girl. 'I love Mull and its little people.'

They had a pleasant enough night and the next morning they went down to the beach to set sail, but when they tried to push the boat out into the water they couldn't shift her an inch.

'I know where we are,' said the young wife from Islay. 'This is the Green Island, and it's an enchanted place. You can't move here for spells.' She told them her mother had given her a little cap as a parting gift, and had told her, if she was ever in a tight corner, to put on the cap and bow her head seven times.

They all climbed into the boat, and the Islay woman put on the cap. She bowed her head, and the sea rose up to her breast. With each bow the water rose higher still – to her neck, to her chin, her mouth, nose, eyes; and when it lapped over the top of her head, *Six Oars* gave a great heave and floated away from the shore of the Green Island and into the fog. It was getting on for evening, and Hidebasket told them to row, and follow the direction in which the birds were flying, as birds head for land at night.

At dawn the fog cleared and they sighted the coast of Mull. As they came close to the shore the boat ran into a narrow gully, and all her oars were broken. After that, the place was called Caolas a' Bhristidh Ràmh – the Narrow Strait of the Broken Oars.

And so they arrived home and told everyone of their adventures.

The King Who Wished to Marry His Daughter

There was a king who was a widower with one daughter. Secretly he vowed to himself that he would only marry again if his new wife could fit into the dead wife's clothes.

One day his daughter was going through her mother's wardrobe, and she came across a dress so beautiful that she had to try it on. It fitted perfectly. She ran to show her father and, as soon as he saw her, he told her that he wanted to marry her. The girl was dreadfully upset. She ran to her nurse in tears, and told her of the king's passion.

'Tell him that you won't marry him until he gets you a dress made of swansdown,' said the nurse. It took the king a year and a day, but he got the dress made – and many of the swans in the kingdom had a chilly winter.

Again the girl ran to her nurse, saying that her father had the dress, and that he was still keen to marry. 'Tell him you won't marry him until he gets you a dress made of bog cotton.' The king went off and, in a year and a day, he came back with the dress, keener than ever to marry. The following year it was a silk gown, stiff with gold and silver and, the year after that, a gold shoe and a silver shoe.

'Tell him,' said the nurse, 'to bring you a kist that will lock on the outside and on the inside, and that can float on water.' When the girl got the kist, she folded up her own clothes and her mother's clothes, and laid them inside it. Then she climbed into the kist herself and asked her father to lock it and put it out to sea, to find out how well it would float. When the kist was in the water, it drifted off, further and further away from the shore, until it was washed up on another shore entirely. A herd boy found it, and tried to break it open, but the girl called to him from inside to fetch his father. The man came and let her out, and took her and the kist back to his house, and it turned out that he was the cattleman for the king of that country.

The girl asked if she might be able to get work in the king's house. 'Not unless you're prepared to work under the cook, as a skivvy,' replied the cattleman. The girl said she would be happy with that, so the cattleman went to ask on her behalf, and she got the job.

On the first Sunday that the girl was in the kitchens, people were leaving for church. They asked if she would be going with them, but she said there was bread to bake, so she would have to stay behind. When everyone had gone she hurried to the cattleman's house, took the swansdown dress out of the kist, and put it on.

The king's son was in church, when a beautiful woman dressed in a swansdown gown walked in and sat facing him. He had never seen anything so gorgeous; he fell for her there and then. But before the sermon was finished, the girl slipped out and went back to get changed, and she was working in the kitchen by the time everyone returned to the big house, all of them talking about the beautiful stranger who had appeared in the church.

The next Sunday it was the same. The girl came to the church, a vision in a dress of bog cotton. The king's son was dazzled all over again, but she was away and back in the kitchens before the sermon was over.

On the third Sunday, after she had made her excuses, the girl went to the cattleman's house and put on the gold shoe, the silver shoe, and the silk dress that was stiff with gold and silver. This time, when she came into the church, the king's son was already sitting in her seat. When she went to sit in the seat where he had been the previous week, she noticed that there were guards posted at all the doors. The girl bolted for the only crack of an exit that she could see. She managed to escape, but one of the guards grabbed the golden shoe off her foot. The king's son took hold of the shoe as if it were the most precious thing he had ever held, and announced to everyone that he would marry whoever it fitted.

There was great competition to become the bride of the king's son. A long queue formed in front of the palace of folk who were desperate to try on the shoe. People were cutting off their toes and heels to make their feet smaller, but no one could get the shoe to fit; and while all this was going on, a little bird sat on top of a high tree singing:

Hoo, hoo, it's not for you
Under the cook is the foot for the shoe

No one had the faintest idea what the bird was singing about. The cook wore size ten boots, and she wasn't the least bit interested in marrying the king's son. The king's son himself was so exhausted by the search that he had to go and lie down. While he was resting, his mother went to the kitchens to see if she could get to the bottom of the mystery. While the queen was there, a grubby little skivvy asked if she could at least have a look at the shoe. 'I won't do it any harm,' she said.

'What makes you think the shoe would fit you, you dirty, ugly creature?' The queen was so indignant, she went straight to her son's bedroom and told him what had happened.

'How do you know it won't fit her?' asked the king's son wearily. 'If it will make her happy, at least let her try the shoe on.'

So the gold shoe was taken down to the kitchens and, as soon as it was put down, it skipped across the flagged floor and hopped straight on to the girl's foot. Never did shoe fit foot more snugly.

'Would you like to see the other one?' the girl asked. She led them to the cattleman's house, and out of the chest she took the silver shoe, as well as the dress made of swansdown, the dress made from bog cotton, and the silk gown stiff with gold and silver. The king's son was more than delighted. A minister was called for, and they were married on the spot.

People of the Hollow Hills

In 1871, during a visit to the island of Tiree in the Inner Hebrides, J.F. Campbell came across a household where there was: '... a cripple idiot boy who is generally supposed to be a changeling. He is often quoted to the Minister as a proof of the fact in which all this Island most firmly believe.'

When Campbell was writing, belief in the *daoine sìth* – the Good People – who we sometimes call fairies, was still strong in rural communities in the West Highlands and the Western Isles. They were an immortal race who lived in a world which was very close to ours, and they had their homes in green mounds or hills which were known as *sìtheanan*. The Good People were notorious for stealing human children, and adults too, and replacing them with one of their own kind – a Changeling. This belief was often used to explain the condition of a disabled child or a child with a degenerative illness – like the boy on Tiree – or to account for a sudden change in a person's demeanour. We still talk of people who are 'away with the fairies'.

Once or twice a year, generally at Hogmanay and Hallowe'en, the door to the *sìthean* would open for a while, and humans could enter. Time inside the green hill ran much slower than time in the world outside, as a fisherman from the island of Iona discovered.

Ferry visitors to Iona arrive at the east side of the island, right next to the village itself. Many choose to go north, by the famous abbey and beyond, but those who head west will pass a green mound at the side of the road. It's sometimes called the Hill of Angels, because St Columba had a vision of angels there, but it is also known to be a fairy dwelling. One evening two young men were coming back from fishing on the west side, when they heard the sound of music in the distance. As they got closer to the *sìthean* they saw a light. The door was open, and there was a party going on inside. One of the men leapt in and joined the dancers without even waiting to lay down the string of fish in his hand. The second was more cautious. He stuck a fish hook in the door before he went in, and only stayed a short time. When he left he pulled the fish hook out, and the door closed, with his pal still inside. When the fisherman got home without his companion he was suspected of foul play, but no one could prove anything, so he was left to his own devices. A year later, when he went back to the mound, the door was open again and his friend was still inside dancing, with the string of fish over his shoulder. The man on the outside stuck a fish hook in the door, as he'd done a year before. When his friend danced closed to him he reached in, grabbed his elbow, and hauled him outside. Then he pulled out the fish hook, and the door slammed shut. Instantly the fish fell from the string and rotted away on the ground, while the dancer collapsed exhausted. He'd been dancing for a whole year even though, inside the green hill, only an evening had passed.

While it's hard for humans to enter the world of the *daoine sìth*, the fairies can easily come and go in our world. Sometimes they are small, like sprites, but they are more likely to be of human size, and are quite capable of having intimate relationships with mortals. For protection against their powers it's useful to possess cold steel – a dirk or a fish hook – and to remember that a sprinkle of urine can dispel fairy enchantment. The stories that follow are entertainments, but they are also guides to overcoming the difficulties and dangers that arise when mortals have to deal with the Good People.

~ THE DUNADD FAIRIES ~

To the north of the Crinan Canal is the Mòine Mhòr – the Great Moss – an area rich in plants and wildlife, which began to form when the sea started to retreat around 5,000 years ago, leaving behind a raised peat bog. Antiquities and legends cluster round the Mòine Mhòr. Rising out of the bog is the rock that is crowned by Dunadd, an Iron Age fort which, in the sixth century, became the power centre for the kings of Dál Riata. The short but steep climb to the top of the fort leads to a horizontal rock face that bears the weather-worn carving of a boar, some writing in Ogham script, and the deep imprint of a human foot. The belief that the placing of a regal foot of flesh and blood into this imprint was a component of a king's coronation seems to go back no further than Victorian times. More plausible is an older tale; that Ossian – son of Finn MacCool, the legendary Irish warrior – had been hunting on the slopes above Loch Fyne, when a cornered stag turned on him. Ossian gave a mighty leap to Rhudle hill, which is not far from Dunadd, and then to Dunadd fort itself, and landed so heavily that he left the mark of his foot in the rock.

There was a farmer of Dunadd who had the Second Sight. He was plagued by visions which came unexpectedly, and which would often show gloomy events, such as funerals, that had still to take place. One evening he was lying in his bed. There was a peat fire burning in the room, and next to the fire was the milk, warming gently so that the cream would be ready for skimming off the next morning. As the farmer watched, a band of fairies came in, carrying a child that they had just stolen, and planning to perform a ritual washing that would make it hard for anyone to take the baby away from them. The farmer had a steel blade under his pillow, to protect himself from evil powers, so he felt fairly safe lying there. As he watched, the fairies began to hunt around, looking for water to wash the baby. When they couldn't find any, they began instead to use the cream from the milk. The little people were so absorbed in their task that they didn't realise how quickly time had passed. Outside in the yard the cockerel crowed, announcing the day's dawning. The fairies picked up the child and hurried back to their green home. They were in such a rush that they left behind a tiny bag, which the farmer confiscated.

Next morning the farmer ordered the milk to be emptied out into the yard. His wife and the servants thought he was mad until the dogs that had lapped up the cream dropped dead on the spot.

The fairies never came back to reclaim their property. The contents of the bag included a little stone spade, which looked a lot like one of the prehistoric flint arrowheads that are sometimes called 'elf shot'. There was also a tiny bowl, for making fairy porridge, and some stone balls. If the spade was placed under the pillow of a person who was ill, the invalid's survival could be predicted by whether or not a sweat broke out on their forehead. Sick cattle could be cured if they were given water to drink from a pail in which the stone balls had been immersed. These magical objects stayed in the farmer's family for many generations and, for all I know, his descendants may still possess them.

And a story from Kintraw, which is fifteen miles or so north of Dunadd, on the other side of the steep pass that leads out of Kilmartin Glen.

A Kintraw farmer's wife had died. On the Sunday after the funeral he went to church with his servants, and left his oldest daughter, who was about ten years old, to look after the other two children. When he returned home, the children told him that their mother had come to visit, and that she had brushed their hair and dressed them. They persisted in the story, and were punished for telling lies, but after church the following Sunday their father was told the same tale. If their mother appeared to them again, he told the children, they should ask her why she had come. A week later the mother did appear for a third time. She told the children that she wasn't dead, but that she had been taken away by the Good People, and was only able to get away for a few hours once a week. If her coffin was opened only a withered leaf would be found inside – and nothing more.

The farmer went to the minister and told him the story, but the minister scoffed at the idea of the *daoine sìth*, and wouldn't

countenance the opening of the wife's coffin. Not long after, the minister himself was found dead, on the side of the green mound that the Kintraw people called the Fairy Hill. It was said that the fairies had taken their revenge on him, for laughing at them.

~ The Smith and the Fairies ~

There was a smith living on Islay. His name was MacEachern, and he had a son who was in his early teens. One day the boy was cheerful and healthy, the next he took to his bed, moping and moaning. At first the smith thought this was no more than typical for someone of his son's age, but as time passed the lad became more and more sullen. His skin took on a yellow tinge, his eyes became large and bright, and the flesh hung off his bones, though he was ravenously hungry all the time.

The smith spent night and day worrying about his son and what would happen to the boy. He lost his enthusiasm for work in the forge, and found it hard even to raise his hammer. He cheered up a little when an old man, a good friend, came in. As the man was known for his wisdom and his knowledge of arcane things, the smith told him about the troubling situation. The old man sat for a while without saying anything, then he told the smith what he believed was happening. 'That's not your son in the bed. He's been taken away by the *daoine sìth* and they've left one of their own in his place.'

The smith knew well enough how the fairies could steal unbaptised babies and leave Changelings in their cots, but he'd never heard of this happening to an older person. He despaired of ever seeing his son again, and asked the man if there was anything that could be done.

'The first thing is to make sure that the creature is definitely not your son. Gather together as many empty eggshells as you can, and take them into the bedroom. Make sure he can see what you're doing. Take the shells to the bucket two at a time, fill them with water and take them over to the fire, pretending that they're really heavy. Then arrange them around the fire as if you're doing something terribly important.'

The smith gathered together his broken eggshells, took them into the bedroom, and began the solemn ritual. It wasn't long before there was a shriek of laughter, and a voice from the bed cried, 'I'm eight hundred years old, and I've never seen anything like it in my life!'

The smith went back to the old man and told him what had happened. 'Just as I thought,' said the old man. 'Your son is being held prisoner in the green hill where the fairies live. Get rid of the creature in the bed as soon as possible, and you have a good chance of getting your boy back. Make a roaring fire next to the bed. When the Changeling asks why you would want to do this, say that he'll find out soon enough, then grab hold of him and throw him into the middle of the flames. If I've made a mistake and it is your son, he'll cry out for your help; but if I'm right, the thing will fly out through the roof.'

The smith did as the old man had told him. He built the raging fire and, when the thing in the bed asked what was going on, the smith took it and threw it into the flames. The Changeling gave a shriek. With a flash, it flew out through the smoke hole in the roof.

The old man told the smith to go on Hallowe'en night to the green hill where the fairies were holding his son, and he would find a door open in the hill's side. He was to take a Bible with him, together with a dirk and a cockerel. There would be the sounds of singing and music from inside the hill, but the smith should keep his chin up, because the Bible would protect him from any harm that the fairies might do to him. He was to put the dirk in the side of the door to stop it closing, and go inside. 'You'll find yourself in a large room, bright and spotlessly clean, and at the far end will be your son, working at a forge. When the fairies ask why you're there, tell them you've come for your boy, and that you won't leave without him.'

When the night of Hallowe'en came round, the smith went out with the Bible, the dirk and the cockerel and made his way to the green hill. In the distance he saw the light from the open door and, as he got closer, he could hear that a party was going on – carousing, and the stamp of feet to the music of the pipes. He got to the hill and looked inside, and there, at the far end of the room, was his son, hammering away over an anvil, sweat flying from his forehead.

The smith stuck his dirk in the door frame and stepped inside. The music stopped and the fairies came towards him. When they saw the Bible he clutched to his chest, their thin smiles turned to sour frowns, for they knew they couldn't touch him. They asked what he wanted. 'I've come for my son. I can see him over there, and I won't leave without him.'

The fairies screeched with laughter, and the racket woke the cockerel, which had been dozing peacefully under the smith's arm. It jumped up on to his head and began to flap its wings, and crowed loudly as if it was dawn.

This made the fairies furious. They took the smith and his son, and threw them out of the green hill. The dirk followed. The moment it hit the ground, the door to the hill slammed shut, and the two mortals were left out in the darkness.

The smith took his son back home. He hoped that the boy would be back to his old self again, but the lad just moped gloomily around. He didn't do any work and he hardly said a word.

A year and a day went by and, one morning, the smith's son was watching his father finishing a sword that had been commissioned by a chieftain. Suddenly he shouted, 'That's not the way you do it!' He grabbed the tools and the sword out of his father's hands, and set to work, and he made a sword that was finer than any seen before in those parts.

After that, father and son worked happily together. Their reputation as master craftsmen spread, and they were never without work again.

~ The Two Sisters ~

The story of the two adventurous brothers, Hidebasket and Skinman, is told in the previous chapter, 'Not Long After the Beginning'. When they returned to Mull, they recounted the experiences of the voyages of *Six Oars*. In return the people told them this story, which had happened when the brothers and their crew were away.

There were two sisters. One was named Mairearad, the other Ailsa. Mairearad loved a fairy man, and was seeing him secretly. She told Ailsa of her clandestine passion, and made her swear not to share the knowledge with anyone else.

'It's as likely to come from my knee as from my lips,' said Ailsa. But she did tell, and the next time the fairy man visited Mairearad he knew he was being spied on. Mairearad never saw him after that. She took to wandering the hills and the hollows, and never went inside a dwelling again. The herdsmen tried to get to her, hoping to persuade her to return home, but they only ever heard a voice, far off, singing a sad song of a sister's betrayal, and of revenge through fairy magic:

Cold is the hearthstone where I had my home
Cold is my father who lies in his tomb
Cold is my bed on the bleak mountain side
Cold is my heart to the sister who lied

In the song, Mairearad wished terrible things for Ailsa:

Hopes turned to ashes, a lifetime of rain
Moths in the kist, rats in the grain
The worm in your heart, lice in your hair
And a withering end to the infants you bear

Sometimes, on moonless nights, Mairearad the wild woman would creep unseen into the township and listen through closed doors to the conversations that went on inside the houses. One of these times, she heard that Ailsa was married, and had got a son who was christened Torquil. Mairearad made up another verse to her song:

Brown haired Torquil, lord of the hill
Torquil the seal hunter, king of the kill
Swinging his sickle out in the corn
The swiftest reaper since Adam was born

When Torquil grew up he did indeed become a celebrated reaper. No one could match him. One autumn he got word that a woman had been seen going into the fields after the reapers returned home, and finishing whatever work they'd been unable to complete. People said she came out of a nearby cairn, and that she could do the work of seven men. Torquil wanted to see this Cairn Girl in action. One evening, he finished work in his own field later than usual. Just as he was leaving he looked back and there she was, by the light of the full moon, beginning her night labours.

Torquil ran to the place where he kept his sickle, and began to reap the next furrow. He called to the woman, 'You're good, but I will overtake you.' When he realised that she was getting further and further ahead, he shouted out, 'Cairn Girl, wait for me, wait for me.'

She called back, 'Brown haired boy, catch up, catch up.'

Torquil was sure he would be able to overtake her, so he carried on until a cloud went in front of the moon and he couldn't see what he was doing. He shouted, 'The moon's gone dark, wait for me, wait for me.'

'I've no other light, catch up, catch up.'

But Torquil couldn't catch up with the Cairn Girl. She was drawing further and further away. He shouted after her a third time, 'I'm tired with the reaping, wait for me, wait for me.'

'I'm climbing the steep hill, catch up, catch up.'

'My sickle needs sharpening, wait for me, wait for me.'

'My sickle wouldn't take down the flowering garlic – catch up, catch up.'

At first light the Cairn Girl reached the head of her furrow and turned to face Torquil. He reached the head of his own furrow and reaped the very last handful of corn, which was called the Harvest Maiden. By tradition, the reaper who cut down the Maiden would take her home as a prize and keep her safe until the next harvest. The reaper behind him, who went home empty handed, would have to take on the care of one of the old, destitute women of the parish as a forfeit.

Torquil stood with his sickle in one hand, and the handful of corn in the other. 'I thank you,' he said. 'You left me the Maiden and saved me from the Old Woman.'

'I did. But you should know how unlucky it is to reap the Maiden so early on a Monday morning.'

It was indeed unlucky. Torquil fell dead in the furrow, and Mairearad's curse was fulfilled.

With a Little Help

In the world of folk tales, aid can come quite unexpectedly, sometimes from surprising helpers. A giant talking bird, an uncharacteristically friendly giant, a band of men with unusual skills, may all pop up to provide assistance, particularly when the hero of a story is at a loss.

There are helpers both supernatural and human in the next three stories, while the Seven Champions who come to the aid of Finn in the first tale are neither quite one nor the other. Finn MacCool was a legendary warrior-hunter who, with his band of followers, the Feinne, was entrusted with the defence of the northern part of Ireland. *The Annals of the Four Masters*, an early seventeenth-century chronicle of Irish history, gives the date of his death as 283. But whether or not he existed historically, many of the stories told about Finn are the stuff of legend, and the tale of Finn MacCool and the Big Young Hero is no exception. Finn's name and exploits, and those of his followers, are associated with hill forts and natural landscape features throughout the Highlands and Islands, particularly in the west. A huge rock pillar close to Dunollie Castle, near Oban, is known as Clach a' Choin, the Dog Stone. Finn is said to have used the rock to tether his favourite hunting dog Bran.

The tale of Peter the Gold comes from the days of the great Atlantic sailing ships. It was known by local families on Iona, and was told in the 1980s to Mairi MacArthur, whose translation from the Gaelic is included here.

MacPhie of Colonsay is a fine example of a Champion. Like Big Malcolm MacIlvain, whose story is told in 'On the Run', he's a travelling trouble-shooter, a sword for hire, prepared to voyage long distances to fight the forces of evil and the denizens of the Otherworld. Both this and the story of Finn share a giant hand, and a dog or two.

– Finn MacCool and the Big Young Hero –

At the end of a good hunting day Finn and his men were resting in the sun, in the shelter of a green hill. They could see everything that was going on, though nobody could see them at all. Finn looked out to sea and there was a ship, heading for the bay below the hill. When the ship reached the shore, a Big Young Hero jumped out, grabbed her by the bows, and hauled her on to the grass. Then he bounded up the hill till he reached the hunting party, and saluted Finn. Though he hadn't the slightest idea who the Hero was, Finn greeted him back and asked where he came from, and what his business was.

'I've sailed through days and nights; through wild winds, rain, hail, sleet and snow to get here. I keep losing my children, and I've been told that you, Finn, are the only man in the world who can end my misfortune.' The Hero made Finn promise on his oath that he wouldn't eat, drink or sleep until he had come looking for the Hero, and found him in the place where he lived. Then the Hero bounded back down the hill. He leaned his shoulder against the boat and heaved it out on to the water. Finn and his men watched as the Hero left in the direction he'd come, until they lost sight of him completely.

This unexpected turn of events made Finn feel very gloomy. The obligation he'd been put under meant that he would have to find the Big Young Hero, or starve to death, but he had no directions and no idea of what was to be asked of him. With a heavy heart he said goodbye to his men, and went down the hill to the place from which the Hero had set sail. When he reached the edge of the sea he started to walk along the beach, and he saw seven men coming to meet him. Finn asked the first of them what skills he had.

'I'm a good Carpenter.'

'How good is that?'

'See that big alder over there? I can make a fair-sized boat from it with three strokes of my axe.'

'That's good enough,' said Finn. He asked the others in turn what their skills were.

The second said he was a good Tracker. Finn asked him how good, and the Tracker said he could follow a wild duck across all of the Seven Seas and back again. 'Good enough for me,' said Finn.

The third man said he was a good Gripper. 'Once I get hold of something, I won't let go until my arms are torn out of their sockets.'

The fourth man said he was a good Climber. 'I can climb a silk thread right up to the stars.'

The fifth man said he was a good Thief. 'I can steal the egg from under a heron, even if she's looking straight at me.'

The sixth man said he was a good Listener. 'I can hear what's being said beyond the very edge of the world.'

The seventh man said he was a good Marksman. 'I can hit an egg as far away as the finest arrow can travel.'

All this talent cheered Finn up. He told the Carpenter to prove his skills. The man went over to the alder and, with three blows of his axe, he made a ship. Finn told the Tracker about the Big Young Hero and which direction he'd taken, and told him to put his talents to work. They all climbed into the boat and set off, with the Tracker at the prow and Finn at the tiller.

They sailed all day – with the Tracker telling Finn to steer this way, or steer that way – and at evening, when the light was fading, they spied land. When they reached the shore they leaped out and pulled the boat up on to the beach. On the hill facing them was a big house. They climbed up towards it and, as they got closer, they saw the Big Young Hero running down to meet them. He threw his arms around Finn's neck. 'My dear sweet man, I knew you'd come.'

'Dear sweet man or not, you gave me no help at all in finding you.'

'That's not true. Didn't I send you these seven splendid Champions?'

They got to the big house, and the Hero told them to go in. A great banquet had been prepared. After they'd eaten, the Big Young Hero came in and spoke to Finn. 'Six years ago, my wife was in labour. As soon as she'd given birth, a huge hand came down the chimney and stole the child away. Three years ago this evening, the same thing happened, and now she's about to give birth again. I was told you were the only man in the world who could help me keep my children, so I'm trusting that this is true.'

Finn's men were tired and sleepy. He told them to stretch out on the floor while he kept watch. He sat by the fire and, every time his eyelids began to close, he roused himself by pushing a hot iron bar into the palm of his hand.

Around midnight the wife of the Big Young Hero gave birth. As soon as the baby was born, a huge Hand came down the chimney. Finn shouted to the Gripper, and the Gripper sprang to his feet and grabbed hold of the Hand. The Hand pulled one way and the Gripper pulled the other, back and forth, until the Gripper was so far up the chimney that only his feet could be seen. Then the Gripper gave a mighty tug on the Hand, and the arm to which the Hand was attached came out of its socket and dropped on the floor. Immediately another Hand came down the chimney, closed round the child, and back up it went, with the baby in its grasp.

They were more than sorry to have lost the baby, but Finn said that they wouldn't give up, and the next morning he and the Seven Champions were awake at dawn, and off in search of the owner of the Hand. They got to the beach where they had left the boat, jumped in, and away they went, with the Tracker at the prow and Finn at the tiller. Over the wide sea they sailed, as the Tracker told them to go first this way, and then that, and for the whole day they saw nothing but water. Then, at dusk, Finn spotted a black dot on the horizon, too big to be a bird and too small for an island. They steered towards it. When they got closer they saw that it was a rock, and on the rock was a castle, thatched with eel-skins.

Finn and the Seven Champions landed on the rock and went all around the outside of the castle, but they couldn't see a door or even a window. Then they looked up, and realised that the door was in the roof. They didn't know how to get up to it, as the eel-skin thatch was so slippery, but the Climber said that it wouldn't take him long. In a bound he was on the roof. He peeped in through the door and, when he'd had a good look, he came back down to join the rest of the party.

The Climber said he'd seen a Big Giant lying on a bed, which had a satin sheet and a silk coverlet; the Giant held a baby in the palm of his hand; on the floor, two boys were playing shinty with golden sticks and a silver ball; and there was a massive deer-hound bitch, suckling two pups at the fireside.

Finn said he didn't know how to get them out. 'It won't take me long,' said the Thief. In no time at all he'd brought out the baby, then the two boys who were playing shinty. He went back again for the satin sheet and the silk coverlet, and then a third time for the shinty sticks and the silver ball. Lastly he brought out the two deer-hound pups. While all this was going on, the Giant slept soundly.

Finn and the Seven Champions loaded the spoils into the boat, and set sail away from the rock. They weren't long at sea when the Listener stood up trembling. 'I can hear him, I can hear him!'

Finn asked what it was that he could hear. 'The Giant has just woken up. He realises that he's been robbed, and he's furious. He's told the bitch that if she won't go, he'll go himself, but it's the bitch who's coming.'

They looked behind them and saw the bitch swimming towards them, throwing off red sparks as she ripped through the sea. The men were terrified. They didn't know what to do. Finn told them to throw out one of the pups, as the bitch might see it drowning and go back for it. They threw out the pup, and the bitch did stop to save it. She took it between her jaws, and swam back to the rock.

It wasn't long before the Listener stood up again. He was shaking all over. 'I can hear him, I can hear him! He's telling the bitch to go back, but she's refusing, so he's coming after us himself.'

They looked back and there was the Giant, striding towards them with the water of the sea scarcely above his knees. They didn't know what to do. But Finn had a magic tooth, a tooth of knowledge; if he touched it with his thumb, it would reveal secret information. He put his thumb to the tooth, and learned that the Giant could never be killed, except through a mole that was in the palm of his hand. Finn told this to the Marksman, who assured him that, if he got one glance at that mole, the Giant would be done for.

The Giant reached the side of the ship and raised his hand to take hold of the mast and sink the vessel. The Marksman watched, eagle-eyed. The mole was in full view. The Marksman loosed an arrow which hit the mole and went right through the hand, and the Giant fell back, stone dead into the sea. They were all relieved, for there were no more terrors to overcome. They swung the boat around and returned to the rock, where, for a second time, the Thief stole the second pup. After that, they sailed back to the island of the Big Young Hero. When they got to the beach, they leapt out and hauled the boat on to the sand.

Finn walked up to the big house with everything the Champions had taken from the Giant's castle, the baby in his arms, and the two older sons of the Big Young Hero skipping at his heels. When the Hero and his wife saw their lost family returned, they wept. The Hero asked Finn what he wanted as a reward, and Finn said that he would be content with one of the pups.

There was a great feast of celebration in the House of the Big Young Hero. It went on for a year and a day, and if the last day of it wasn't the best, it certainly wasn't the worst.

And that's how Finn came by Bran, his best hunting dog.

– Peter the Gold –

Peter and another two fellows from Iona were fishing out beyond Erraid, the little island off the south-west tip of Mull. Those that know it say it's a dirty spot there, with a lot of skerries dotted around, very risky for shipping. About midday a heavy mist came down, but they knew just to rest on their oars and wait. When it lifted, what did they see but a big sailing ship heading straight for the Torran Rocks, the worst area of all. It gave them a fright. But when the ship came closer the skipper hailed them, asking if anyone could come on board to help guide his vessel to safety – and that he'd be well paid for his trouble.

Peter threw a rope, jumped aboard and soon the ship was out of danger. But as the saying goes – 'a good promise and a bad pay' – rather than handing over any money, the skipper cut the small boat's rope. Soon, both it and Peter's companions were left well astern. And the skipper told Peter they were making for America and that he would have to work as a crew member. The poor chap had no option but to put up with it; he got very little food, had just a corner of the deck for shelter and, at times, thought he'd never see land again.

When they reached America, Peter was put ashore with no money, with no proper clothing and with barely a word of English. He didn't know what to do but began to walk back and forth along the quayside. A lad spotted him and, realising something was wrong, spoke to him. But Peter clearly didn't understand much English and so the lad beckoned him towards an office opposite the quay. Inside was a gentleman who greeted Peter in fluent Gaelic and asked warmly how the voyage had gone because – guess what? – this was the owner of the ship! Peter told him, word for word, what had happened since going out to fish off Iona months before.

The owner listened in silence. He then whistled for the lad and asked him to fetch the skipper. When the skipper arrived the owner said, 'Do you recognise this man?'

'Yes,' said the skipper.

'Where did you see him?' asked the owner.

'He was part of my crew and I put him ashore on the quay with the rest,' answered the skipper.

The owner then turned sharply and repeated, word for word, Peter's story, lambasting the skipper from the top of his head to the soles of his feet. 'Look here,' he said. 'For this shabby behaviour I want you to put five hundred English pounds on the table within two hours, for Peter. If you don't, I'll put you in prison till your teeth rot.'

The owner then took Peter to a nearby shop and bought him clothes, shoes and everything else he needed. The skipper reappeared and counted out five hundred gold coins on the table – but then said that he would take Peter back to Scotland. 'No you won't!' said the owner. 'Peter will sail back with me in another ship.'

Peter made a special bag which he tied over his shoulder and that's how he carried the gold home. The owner laughed and at once nicknamed him Pàraig an Oir, the Gaelic for Peter the Gold. Eventually Peter reached Greenock in the Firth of Clyde, got a boat from there to Mull and walked the thirty or so miles to Fionnphort, opposite Iona, the bag still on his back. He got safely to his own fireside more than a year after disappearing. No one had expected him to return.

They say that the heavy bag left a dent in his shoulder till the day his old grey head was laid to rest in the Reilig Odhrain. And before he died, others remembered, Peter would sometimes take a gold coin from the bag and hold it out in his palm, to show the island children what he had once brought back from a long day's fishing.

~ MacPhie's Black Dog ~

Mac Mhic Ailein of Arisaig – the Son of Alan's Son – Laird of Moidart, was out hunting one day in his deer forest when he saw in the distance a stag whose antlers were like the branches of a vast tree. When he raised his gun and took sight down the barrel, the stag became a beautiful woman, and when he lowered the barrel the woman turned back into a stag. Mac Mhic Ailein was young and a bachelor, and the look of the woman roused him. He lifted the gun again, and advanced slowly towards her until he was close enough to leap forward and grab hold of her in her human form.

'I want to keep you with me forever,' said Mac Mhic Ailein. 'I'll never marry anyone but you.'

'Mac Mhic Ailein, that's a bad idea,' the woman replied. 'I'm not your kind. I'll ruin you. You'll need to provide me with a whole cow for each day I stay with you.'

But Mac Mhic Ailein was besotted beyond reason. 'You can have two cows each day if you want them,' he said. And so they married. But it wasn't long at all before Mac Mhic Ailein's herd started to thin out, and he began to realise what a terrible mistake he had made. When he tried to send his new wife away, she wouldn't leave, so he went and told his troubles to an old man who he relied upon for advice. The old man told Mac Mhic Ailein that the only person who could rid him of the woman was MacPhie of Colonsay.

A letter was sent to MacPhie. As soon as he read it, he set sail for Arisaig. Mac Mhic Ailein explained the situation, and MacPhie told him to kill the cow for the woman that day as usual, and to put her to eat at one end of the room, with MacPhie at the other. The dinner was served, and MacPhie and the woman began to eat.

'What's the news with you, my Charmer?' MacPhie asked of her.

'What's that to you, Brian Boru?'

'It's been a long time. I remember you when you kept company with Finn MacCool, and when you went on the run with Diarmid.'

'I remember you, Brian Boru, riding an old black horse, chasing from broch to broch, when your fairy girlfriend was leading you a merry dance.'

'I know what she is,' MacPhie shouted out. 'She's as old as the hill that she came out of. Fetch the men and dogs, and drive her back inside.'

Every man and every dog in Arisaig went off in pursuit of the woman. The trail led them out to the Point, but when they got there, there was no sign of her.

MacPhie's work was done, so he went back to Colonsay. One day he was out hunting, and it grew dark when he was still a good way from home. He saw a light in the distance and headed straight for it. There were several men sitting in the house, and among them was an old, grey-haired fellow. 'Come closer, MacPhie,' said the old man. As MacPhie approached the man, a beautiful bitch came up to him, with a litter of pups. One of the pups was pure black, and the finest dog MacPhie had ever seen.

'That dog is mine,' he said.

'You can't have it,' said the old man. 'You're welcome to take any of the others.'

'He's the one I want, only him.'

'In that case you can have the dog, but listen carefully; you'll only get one day's service out of him, though it will be worth waiting for.' The old man told MacPhie to come back in so many days time. When he returned, the men handed over the dog, and told him again that it would only give him one day's service.

The Black Dog turned out to be such a beautiful, sleek animal that everyone who saw it remarked on its good looks; but whenever MacPhie went out hunting and called to the dog, it would go as far as the threshold, then turn and slink back inside the house and lie down in its usual place. Friends who visited told MacPhie that the dog was a waste of food and space, and that he should

kill it. '*Thig là a' choin duibh fhathast* – the Black Dog's day will come in time,' was all MacPhie would say.

Sixteen young gentlemen came over from Islay and asked MacPhie to go hunting with them on Jura. There was no one living on the island at the time, and it was full of red and roe deer. The hunting was incomparable, and there was shelter, the Big Cave, where parties could stay overnight.

The boat was ready to take MacPhie and the sixteen young gentlemen over the Sound. As they left the house they all called to the Black Dog. He went as far as the door, but wouldn't go any further. 'You should shoot that cur,' the gentlemen told MacPhie.

'The Black Dog's day hasn't come yet.'

When they reached the shore a wind rose up, too strong for them to get across the bay, so they returned to the house. Next morning they made to leave again, and again the Black Dog refused to go.

'Kill that dog, MacPhie.'

'I will not kill him. Sure enough, the Black Dog's day will come.'

Next morning the weather was even worse, and once again they couldn't get over to Jura. 'That dog knows something we don't,' said the gentlemen.

'He knows,' MacPhie told them, 'that his day will come.'

On the third day the weather was calm and clear. They started off for the harbour, and never said a word to the Black Dog. When they were about to embark, one of the men called out that the Black Dog was coming. It raced past them, snarling, and with a great leap it was the first to board the boat. 'The Black Dog's day is getting closer,' said MacPhie.

When they reached Jura they took their supplies and bedding to the Big Cave and slept there for the night. They spent the next day hunting, though the Black Dog wouldn't go with them.

The party returned late to the cave. They built a fire and cooked a meal by the light of the torches that were placed around the walls. The cave had a hole in the roof; it was big enough for a man to climb through, and it let out the smoke from the fire.

After supper, the young gentlemen lay down. While MacPhie stood with his back to the fire, warming his legs, each of them in turn said how much he wished his sweetheart was there.

'I'm happier that my wife is safe at home,' said MacPhie. He looked towards the cave entrance and saw a band of young women coming in, sixteen of them. The torches went out, and the only light came from the fire. The women went over to where the young men were lying. MacPhie couldn't hear a sound, and it was too dark to see just what was going on. Then one of the women stood up and came towards MacPhie. She clenched her fists and bared her teeth, and it looked as if she was going to spring at him, but the Black Dog came between them. The hairs on his neck bristled, and he leapt at her. The women headed for the cave entrance and the Black Dog drove them out into the night. Then he came back, and lay down at his master's feet. For a while there was a great silence, and then the earth began to shake. A hand came down through the hole in the roof and started to grope around, searching for MacPhie. The Black Dog jumped up at the hand, and sank his teeth into the flesh between the shoulder and the elbow. Whatever the creature was that the hand belonged to, it tried to shake off the Black Dog, but the hound clung on, chewing relentlessly, until the arm dropped on to the floor of the cave.

The owner of the arm withdrew. Once more the whole cave shook, and MacPhie feared the roof would fall in on his head. He was even more fearful when the Black Dog ran out of the cave, and left him alone to face whatever further terrors the night might cast up.

Dawn came, and the Black Dog returned to the Big Cave, and lay down at MacPhie's feet. MacPhie rested his hand on its head. 'Black Dog,' he said, and within a couple of minutes, the dog was dead.

MacPhie looked around and saw that not a single one of the sixteen young gentlemen was left alive. He took the hand, and went back to Colonsay alone. He showed the hand as evidence of what he had been through. No one on the island had seen anything like it.

A boat was sent to Jura to bring back the bodies from the cave, and that was the end of the Black Dog's day.

When Reason Sleeps

Legends and folk tales are packed with magic: bannocks run, a bear speaks Gaelic, a giant hand steals babies. The next stories, with their wizards and witches, provide grand entertainment, and they embody the exciting, and sometimes terrifying, suspicion that the physical world, and how we perceive it, can be manipulated by supernatural means.

It might seem strange that a Christian saint should be given a place here, but the *Life* of St Columba, who is the subject of the first story, sees him pitted against the Pictish wizards, and winning hands down. Columba's name is firmly linked to the island of Iona, which is just off the west coast of Mull, and now a site of pilgrimage for Christians from all over the world; but his first choice of a base when he came over from Ulster was the fertile island of Lismore. Lismore is in the mouth of Loch Linnhe, sandwiched between Mull and the Argyll mainland, and in many ways a more suitable place than Iona for establishing a proselytising monastic community. Legend has two Irish missionaries, Columba and Moluag, sculling towards the Lismore coast in their hide-covered boats, on the understanding that whichever of the two touches land first should set up there. Moluag, realising that he is lagging behind, cuts off his little finger, throws it to the shore, and so wins the race. Port Moluag, where he landed, still bears his name.

If this happened at all, it was probably in 562, when Moluag was around forty years old. He trained in Bangor, County Down, where he is said to have known the celebrated Brendan the Navigator. Moluag had cells in his name in Mull, Tiree, Skye and Raasay, and his mission took him as far north as Iceland. His bell and crozier still survive, and by the side of the main road that runs the length of Lismore is 'Moluag's Chair', a natural rock seat which has powers to heal those who sit in it, and is particularly efficacious for curing rheumatism.

– Columba's Adventures in the Great Glen –

From at least the sixth century, as Christianity spread, Irish missionaries crossed the sea to the north of Scotland. The best known of these adventurers is Colum Cille, St Columba – the Dove of the Church – who founded the monastery on Iona. Many stories have been told about him over the centuries – for instance that he was in self-exile, as the result of what was essentially a copyright dispute which had led to a bloody battle, and that he wouldn't settle until he found a place far enough away from Ireland that its coast could no longer be seen. More certain is that he was the son of a powerful Donegal family, and that he came to Iona at a time when that part of north-west Britain was already under Irish occupation, with the Kingdom of Dál Riata having been established there over a hundred years previously.

In his efforts to spread the word of the Gospel, Columba hoped to convert the pagan Picts to Christianity and, some time after 565, he made a legendary visit to the court of the Pictish king Bridei, son of Mailcon, who is believed to have lived close to where Inverness is today, perhaps on the site of Urquhart Castle by Loch Ness, or in the hill fort of Craig Phadraig.

In those times people were accustomed to making long and difficult journeys both by land and by water, so the journey Columba and his companions made was perhaps less daunting than it might seem to us today, though it was still a bold undertaking. We don't know what route they followed from Iona to the mainland, in what would likely have been a curragh, a wooden-framed boat covered with animal hides. They probably sailed round the south coast of Mull, then over the Sound of Mull and into the mouth of Loch Linnhe. Then they would have continued up the Great Glen, along the waterways of Loch Lochy, Loch Oich and Loch Ness, carrying the boat over the few miles of land between the lochs.

The story, recorded a hundred years after Columba's death by Adomnán, 9th abbot of Iona and Columba's biographer, begins substantially when the party of monks arrived at Bridei's fortress for the first time. Columba had climbed the steep slope to the gates of the fort. The king was well aware that he had visitors, but decided not to let them in. Columba, after he had been kept waiting for a good while, realised that he was being snubbed. He made the sign of the cross and then, when he knocked on the gates, the bolts flew back and the gates swung open. The king had been watching from his quarters inside the compound. When he saw what had happened, he hurried down to greet the Irish visitors. After that, Bridei always treated Columba with great respect.

There was no such respect from the king's magicians, whose leader, Broichan, was also Bridei's foster father. Not long after Columba had arrived at Bridei's fortress, he and his companions were at Vespers outside the compound, when Broichan and the other magicians came along and started to make a racket, trying to drown out the sounds of prayer. When he was singing psalms, Columba could project his voice for a thousand paces, even though, to those close to him, its volume was no louder than normal. On this occasion he began to sing the 44th Psalm, and the chanting resounded like a peal of thunder, scaring the wits out of Bridei and his people, and utterly dampening the efforts of the wizards.

There were many exciting moments for the monks who accompanied Columba on his mission to the Picts. On one occasion the saint had to cross the river Ness. When he arrived on the far bank of the river he came upon the funeral of a local man who, while he was swimming, had been attacked and killed by a water beast. Some of the man's friends had gone out in a boat to rescue him, but they were too late to save his life, though they'd managed to haul his mangled corpse back to land. Columba astonished everybody by telling one of the monks, whose name was Luigne, to swim across the river and fetch back a dinghy that was on the other side. Luigne stripped down to his tunic and dived in. When he was halfway across, the monster, which was skulking on the riverbed and hoping it could find more prey, felt the water rippling above. It rose up with a terrible roar, just a pole's length from the swimmer. The onlookers gasped, monks and pagans alike, but Columba raised his hand and made the sign of the cross. 'Go back,' he called to the monster, 'and leave this man be.'

The terrified monster retreated so quickly it looked as if it had been hauled away by ropes. Luigne finished his journey to the opposite bank and brought back the dinghy, and even the local people, pagans as they were, were impressed by the power of the Christian God.

After Columba had been a few days in the province of the Picts, a man who had listened to his teachings through the words of a translator had converted to Christianity, along with the rest of his family. Almost immediately, one of his sons began to suffer terrible pain, and it became clear that the boy was going to die. When they saw this, Bridei's magicians began to sneer that their Gods were more powerful than the Christian God, and to reproach the parents for the mistake they had made in converting.

Columba heard what had happened. He went with his companions to the house, and was told that the boy had already died. He comforted the parents and asked where the body was. The boy's father led Columba to the building, and he went alone into the room where the corpse lay, while a big crowd gathered outside. Columba knelt by the boy and prayed, as tears rolled down his cheeks. Then he stood and looked directly at him, and told him to get up and walk. The boy's eyelids flickered and life returned to his body. Columba took his hand and led him out. The boy walked with shaky steps to his parents, and the crowd gave a great shout of jubilation.

Columba discovered that Broichan, the head magician, kept an Irish slave girl. The saint asked him to release the girl, but Broichan refused. In front of King Bridei, Columba told Broichan that, if he didn't let the slave girl go free before the party set off back for Iona, Broichan wouldn't have long to live.

The monks went down to the banks of the river Ness, where Columba picked up a white stone. He told his companions to mark it closely, because in the future it would cure many a sick heathen. Then he said, 'Broichan has just been struck by an angel from heaven. The glass he was about to drink from has shattered in his hand. He can barely breathe, he's near to death. If we wait here a while, two messengers will come from the king. They'll say what has happened, and ask us to go and help, for Broichan is dying. This has given Broichan a timely shock, and now he'll be willing to give up the slave girl.'

Columba had hardly finished speaking when the monks heard the sound of horses' hooves. It was the king's messengers. They told everything that had happened, just as Columba had predicted – the broken cup, the seizure, the willingness to give up the girl – and that the king had sent them to ask for help to restore Broichan to health.

Columba blessed the white stone and handed it to two of the brothers. He told them to give it to the king, who should dip it in water. If Broichan promised to release the girl, and drank the water, he would recover. If he changed his mind, however, he would die there and then.

Miraculously, when the stone was dipped into water, it floated like an apple or a nut. Broichan drank and was cured, and the slave girl was handed over to Columba. The white stone became one of Bridei's most precious possessions, and many sick people were cured by drinking the water that it had empowered – though, strangely, if an attempt was made to cure someone whose natural time had come, it would be impossible to find the stone. This is what happened on the day Bridei died. The stone vanished and was never seen again.

Broichan never gave up challenging or provoking Columba. One day he asked the saint when he planned to return to Iona. 'Since you ask,' replied Columba, 'we'll be leaving tomorrow morning.'

'I don't think that will be possible,' said Broichan, 'because we're going to conjure up a mist and a wind to stop you.' Columba answered that the enterprise would be in the hands of God, and there the matter was left.

The next morning a large crowd gathered as Columba went down to the head of the loch. Bridei's magicians were smugly delighted, because a dense fog covered the waters of the loch, and a stormy wind blew from the very direction in which the monks needed to travel. In the middle of the tempest Columba called on Christ, and climbed into the boat that had been prepared for him. He ordered the hesitant sailors to raise the sail, and the crowd of onlookers watched as it took off, swift as a bird, straight into the prevailing wind. It wasn't long before the wind turned, and a gentle breeze carried Columba and the brothers safely along the first leg of their journey back to Iona and home.

– A Ceilidh Story –

In the days before radio and television, before computers and mobile phones, before video games and streaming, people would meet in the evenings to gossip and sing, tell stories and jokes, ask riddles and play a little music; they would often take with them some domestic work such as darning or sewing, or spinning with the drop spindle. In the parts of Scotland where Gaelic was spoken, a gathering like this would be called a *ceilidh*, and the place where it happened would be well known in the community. It could be someone's house, but it might also be another important location: a smithy for instance, a mill, or a kiln for drying corn.

On the south-west coast of Mull there was such a kiln, a place where men and boys gathered to tell stories. They sat in a row around the fire and the owner of the kiln began with his story, followed by the others in turn. The rule they had – their 'law' – was that everyone there, without exception, should contribute a tale.

On one occasion a young man from another district was present at the session. He didn't know the house rules, and, when it came to his turn, he had no story to tell. The regulars were outraged at this flouting of protocol. Blows were close to being struck, when the owner suggested that the young man go outside to put some straw in a hole in the wall, as it was letting in the wind.

The lad stepped out into the dusk, glad to be away from the prickly atmosphere inside the kiln. There was indeed a strong wind and, when he looked out to sea, he saw that a ship was being driven dangerously close to the rocks. The boy ran down to the shore and found a small boat, pushed it out, and began to row towards the ship in distress, but the gale caught hold of his little vessel and dragged him out to sea, past Colonsay, Jura and Islay, and over to the north coast of Ireland.

The young man was cast up in the mouth of a creek, near to a cottage that was on a hill above the shore. When he enquired at the cottage, he found an old woman and a young girl living there. The old woman's husband, the father of the girl, had died a few weeks before. He had been a fisherman, and now his boat was idle.

The lad from Mull got on well with the old woman, and particularly well with the girl. He knew how to fish too, and so it seemed sensible for him to stay there, marry the daughter, and take over the management of the boat.

The young couple made a good partnership, and it wasn't so long before their first child was born. Quite quickly they had three more children, and the house became filled with the sounds of a happy family, working and playing and eating together. Then one evening the Mull man was out fishing when a great storm rose up, and his boat was blown back over the sea, past Islay, Jura, and Colonsay, to the very place in Mull that he had left all those years before. He climbed the hill to the kiln, which was still there above the beach. When he went in, he was astonished to see the same band of men and boys, sitting in just the same places, and none of them looking a year, or even a day older.

The owner of the kiln asked where he had been, and the young man told of the storm, the voyage to Ireland, his wife and four children. 'Well, at last you have a story to tell,' said the owner. The others started to laugh, but the owner hushed them, saying that the lad had been under a spell, and that his experiences had all been a vision conjured up by magic. That may have been true, but it didn't stop him mourning the wife and children who were as real to him as if they'd been flesh and blood.

People say that the owner of the kiln was a master of the black art, and was himself responsible for the young man's vision, but that surely is an old wives' tale.

THE RED BOOK OF APPIN

The Red Book of Appin was a legendary *grimoire* – a book of spells – which was held in the coastal district that was the location of the notorious Appin murder, an inspiration for Robert Louis Stevenson's novel *Kidnapped*. Hector Urquhart, writing in the 1850s, heard the story of the Red Book as he was walking up Glen Fyne:

> ... I overtook an old man who was carting coals up to the Lodge. 'Good day to you, John.' 'Good day to yourself,' says John. From good days to showery days, I asked John if there was any virtue in iron against witchcraft or fairy spells. 'Indeed, and that's what there is,' says John ... 'On a certain year and me a young lad, all our cows lost the milk, one after one; we guessed what was wrong with them, and my big brother lost no time in going to Appin, to consult the man of the RED BOOK. He no sooner entered his house than the man told him what moved him from home. "It's your own neighbour's wife," says he, "that spoilt your cows; she is this moment in your house, inquiring whether you went from home today, and where did you go to; and to make it double sure to you, that it's her who spoilt your cows, she will meet you under the lintel of your door coming out as you are going in. Go you now home, and take a shoe of an entire horse, and nail it to your byre door; but let no living person know of it."'
>
> My brother came home, and as the man of the red book told him, this identical woman met him on the threshold as he was going in to the house. I do not know how he managed to get hold of the laird's stallion, but the shoe was nailed on our byre door before sunrise next morning, so our cows had plenty milk from that day forth.

The old man, John, told Hector Urquhart how the Red Book came to be in that part of Argyll. There was a man who lived in Appin who took in an orphan boy. When the boy grew old enough he would be sent out to mind the cattle, and one day he was alone on the hill when a gentleman came up, well dressed and well spoken.

'I'm in need of a servant, and you look like just the lad for the job. If you come and work for me you'll get plenty to eat and drink, a fine suit of clothes, and a good wage into the bargain.'

The boy liked the idea of the high life, but he told the gentleman that he would have to ask his master first, since the master had taken the lad in when he had nowhere to go, and had looked after him well. The gentleman seemed anxious to get the business over with, but the boy insisted that the master must be consulted.

'Well then,' the gentleman said, 'you had better at least put your name in the book.' And he pulled out a large red book from under his cloak. Again the boy refused even to say what his name was until the master had been told.

'In that case, since you refuse my generous offer, go and talk to your master, and meet me tomorrow evening at sunset with your decision.'

The boy went back home and told the master about his encounter with the fine gentleman, and what had been discussed.

'You did right to tell me,' the master said, 'and you did right not to put your name in his book. For all his swanky clothes and fancy talk, he's the last person you'd ever want to be working for. Since you agreed to meet him, you should keep your word, but listen to what I tell you and do everything I say.'

The master gave the boy a sword, and told him to be at the agreed place a good while before sunset. When he got there he was to use the sword to draw a circle around him in the name of the Trinity, and then make a cross in the middle of the circle. The boy should stand on the cross and not budge until sunrise, whatever happened.

'He'll try and entice you out of the circle to sign the book, but stay put. Ask him to hand the book to you and, once you've got it, don't let him have it back.'

The boy arrived in good time, and made his circle with the sword. He stood on the cross and waited. The sun had just gone down when the gentleman came walking briskly up out of the shadows of the glen. He took out the book.

'You've made your decision? Will you sign?'

'I've talked to my master, and I will sign.'

'Come out of the circle then. The book's ready and open.'

'I won't come out. Give the book to me here.'

The gentleman did everything he could to lure the boy out. He offered him gold and silver, jewels, castles and princesses. At last he held out the book and, as soon as it crossed the magic circle, it flew from his hand. The boy stretched out, grabbed the book, and gripped it under his armpit.

When the gentleman saw that the boy had no intention of putting his name in the Red Book he flew into a fury. There was a sickening smell of brimstone as smoke and flames came out of his mouth and nostrils. His whole form began to quiver and to take on different shapes; first as a red-eyed horse, then as a huge, bristling cat, and then as a nameless monstrosity, he whirled around the outer edge of the circle, trying constantly, and failing constantly, to break in and take the boy. All night he kept this up, as the boy stood terrified but steadfast, until a sliver of daylight appeared on the horizon. With a desperate screech the gentleman turned himself into a raven and flew away, back to whatever place he'd come from.

When the sun was up the boy ran home as fast as he could, and gave the book to his master. And that's how the Red Book came to Appin.

THE MULL WITCHES

These events are said to have taken place towards the end of the sixteenth century. The story begins in Spain.

One night, the King of Spain's daughter, whose name was Viola, dreamt of the most handsome man she had ever seen, awake or asleep. She set her heart on finding him, wherever in the world he might be, so she had a boat fitted out and took to the sea. Princess Viola had no luck in her quest until she came to Tobermory, on the Isle of Mull, where she found her man. He was the powerful MacLean of Duart, and he needed no encouragement to repay Viola's affections in kind.

MacLean's wife got to hear of the goings-on. She decided to take revenge on the princess, and hired a Lowlander called Smollett to blow up the Spanish ship. Smollett managed to get on board, and lit a long fuse to the magazine before making his getaway. It must have been a very long fuse, because he put twelve miles between himself and Tobermory before the ship went up. The cook was blown to a place called Srongarve, where there's still a cleft in the rock called Uamh Chòcaire – the Cook's Cave. The princess landed way out in the Sound of Mull, and she was buried in the graveyard at Lochaline, over on the mainland.

Revenge begat reprisal. Viola's father, the King of Spain, sent a Captain Forrest to Tobermory, with the purpose of taking the right breast off every woman in Mull. When news of this reached the island, the Lady of Duart called for the help of Doideag, the Mull witch with the frizzy hair. Doideag in turn summoned her two sisters: Ladhrag Thiristeach – the Hoofed One of Tiree – and a' Ghlaisrig Ileach – the Islay Hag. The three witches cooked up a spell to whip up a wind, which entailed the raising and lowering of a quern stone on a rope slung over a beam in Doideag's house.

What a storm it was! Trees were uprooted, heather flew like rain, and the thatch of Doideag's house was ripped clean off. But Tobermory harbour was such a sheltered spot that the water there remained unruffled, and Captain Forrest's ship was quite untouched by the tempest.

The witches gave up their storm-making and wondered what else they could try. 'We need to send word to Gormshùil Mhòr a Lochabar,' said Doideag. The Great Blue-eyed One of Lochaber was a powerful woman. When she got to Mull she set to work, gathering together every able-bodied cat on the island, and maybe cats from other islands as well.

When the feline army was assembled, the Great Blue-eyed One spoke secret words. Captain Forrest and his crew were preparing to go ashore and begin their dreadful mission, when one of them noticed a cat, perched at the very end of the topmost yardarm. Soon it was joined by another cat, and another, until all the yards were crowded with them, and they sat, glaring down at the sailors. On another part of the island, the Great Blue-eyed One gave a command, and in Tobermory harbour the cats launched themselves, like a murder of crows, down on to the sailors. They bit, they clawed, and they tore, until not a man was left alive. Then they streamed down into the belly of the ship, and chewed big holes in the wood of the hull. The water gushed in, and the boat sank to the bottom of Tobermory harbour. What became of the cats, I have no idea.

TELLERS OF TALES

In the latter half of the nineteenth century, when many of these Argyll tales were gathered, the collectors understandably believed that their first duty was to record the stories themselves, before they were made extinct by the rapid social changes that were taking place. This in itself was a huge task, as what were sometimes very long texts had to be taken down by hand from the storyteller's dictation. Still, there are some accounts which give fascinating portraits of these earlier tellers, and two are included below, prefacing 'The Tale of the Soldier' and 'The Girl and the Dead Man'.

There is also a portrait of a storyteller whose life spanned virtually the whole of the twentieth century. John Campbell was born on Iona in 1905. He died aged 94 in the house where he had lived most of his life, near Bunessan in the Ross of Mull. A native Gaelic speaker, he learned story and song of both Mull and Iona from an older generation, and composed many songs and verse himself. Mairi MacArthur first met Johnnie in the mid-1980s during her research into Iona at the School of Scottish Studies in Edinburgh. Below she describes his storytelling style and gives her own translation of 'The Battle of the Thumbs'.

The story of 'Conall Yellow Claw' was recorded in 1859 by the Islay schoolmaster Hector MacLean from the blind fiddler James Wilson. It fits perfectly here, as it is a story about storytelling, of which Conall is a master in the tradition of Scheherazade.

~ The Tale of the Soldier ~

This story was taken down around 1859 from John MacDonald, described as a 'travelling tinker', by gamekeeper Hector Urquhart. Urquhart was one of the collectors who helped John Francis Campbell gather material for *Popular Tales of the West Highlands*. Campbell himself met John MacDonald, and described him as:

> ... a character; he is about fifty years of age; his father, an old soldier, is alive and about eighty; and there are numerous younger branches; and they were all encamped under the root of a tree in a quarry close to Inveraray, at Easter 1859.
>
> The father tells many stories, but his memory is failing. The son told me several, and I have a good many of them written down. They both recite; they do not simply tell the story, but act it with changing voice and gesture, as if they took an interest in it, and entered into the spirit and fun of the tale. They belong to the race of 'Cairds', and are as much nomads as the gipsies are.
>
> The father, to use the son's expression, 'Never saw a school'. He served in the 42d [Regiment – the Black Watch] in his youth. One son makes horn spoons, and does not know a single story; the other is a sporting character, a famous fisherman, who knows all the lochs and rivers in the Highlands, makes flies, and earns money in summer by teaching Southerns to fish. His ambition is to become an under-keeper.

It was difficult to write down MacDonald's stories, as he found it impossible to keep still. When he was telling 'The Brown Bear of the Green Glen' – included in 'Bannocks and Banquets' – Campbell records that '... the wandering spirit of the man would not let him rest to dictate his story. They had to move to an outhouse and let him roam amongst the shavings, and swing his arms ...'

Here is John MacDonald's 'The Tale of the Soldier':

There was an old soldier by the name of John, and he had deserted from the army. He went to the top of the hill that overlooked the town where the regiment was stationed. 'Old Clootie can take me away on his back if I ever return here!' he said.

John came to a big house. He told them that he was an old soldier, and asked if he could get lodgings for the night. The gentleman, who had a mischievous air about him, said, 'You certainly look like a brave man, old soldier. I wonder how brave you really are. There's a castle up the road at the side of the wood. You can spend the night there. I'll let you have a pipe and baccy, a good drop of whisky, and a Bible to read; and if you stick it out, I'll give you a hundred pounds in the morning. By the way, some time in the night you may get a visit from my father.'

John got his supper at the big house and went along to the castle. He built a good fire and sat down beside it. Everything was still and quiet until midnight, when in came two red-haired women, carrying a coffin between them. They dumped the coffin down by the fire, and were away out of the door. John kicked in the end of the coffin with his heel and groped about inside. His fingers touched two icy feet. He tugged on the feet, and out of the coffin slid the corpse of an ancient man, wrinkled and scabby-scalped, with worms crawling in and out of his eye sockets.

John sat the corpse up in the chair by the fire, and put the pipe and the whisky in its hands, but the dead man let them both fall. 'Poor old fellow,' said John, 'you're freezing.' John went to bed and left the dead man to warm himself by the fire. Then, at cock crow, the corpse rose and shuffled out of the room.

The gentleman called round at first light. 'Did you manage to get a good night's sleep, John?'

'Oh yes, indeed I did. It would take more than your father to frighten me.'

'Well done, John. If you spend another night in the castle, you'll get the usual. You'll get the pipe and baccy, the dram and the Bible, and two hundred pounds from me in the morning.'

'I'll take you up on that,' said John; and it was the same as the night before. John was sitting in front of the roaring fire when, in the dead of night, in came three red-haired women. They threw the coffin they were carrying down at the side of the

fire, and hot-footed it out of there. John knocked in the end of the coffin and, as he pulled out the old man, a couple of toes came away in his hand. John threw the toes on the fire, and sat the corpse up in the chair. He put the pipe and baccy, and the drink, in the dead man's hands, but the corpse dropped them, just as he had the previous night. 'Poor old chap,' said John, 'you're cold as ice. But if I come back tomorrow night, and the same thing happens, you'll have to pay for any breakages.' John went to bed and, at cock crow, the corpse rose and hobbled out.

The gentleman dropped by early in the morning. 'Did you get a good night's sleep, John?'

'Couldn't have slept sounder. It would take more than that old galoot, your father, to disturb my slumbers.'

'I'll give you three hundred pounds if you stick it out again tonight,' said the gentleman.

It went just as it had on the previous two nights. John was in the castle, toasting himself in front of the fire, when in came the red-haired women, four of them this time. They dumped the coffin next to him and were away. John kicked in the end of the coffin, and, while he was pulling out the corpse, one of the feet came off in his hand. He threw the foot on the fire, sat the corpse up in the chair, put the pipe and baccy in one of its hands and the dram in the other. The dead man let them fall, the pipe broke and the glass smashed, and the baccy and whisky went all over the floor.

'Well,' said John, 'enough is enough. This time I'm afraid you'll have to pay me for the damage.' He took the belt from his knapsack, and used it to strap the corpse to his side, then he got into bed, with the dead man next to him.

At first light the cock crowed. 'I must leave now,' said the corpse, 'please let me go.'

'Not until you've paid for what's been broken.'

Beneath the house, the corpse told John, there was a cellar full of drink, tobacco and pipes, another cellar with a cauldron full of gold, and a third with a crock of silver. 'Those red-haired women who brought me in,' it gibbered, spitting out a tooth or two. 'I took cattle from them when they had nothing else left, and now they're punishing me. Please go and tell my son that I can't take the torment any longer. Tell him to pay the women for the cows, and to treat the poor with more kindness from now on. You and he can divide the gold and silver between you, but be sure to give plenty to the poor folk as well. And you can have my old girl to marry, for there's a bit of life left in her yet. If you do all these things, I'll be able to rest in peace at last.'

John untied the belt, and the corpse climbed out of bed and hopped off back to the grave. When the gentleman called round, John told him all that had been said, though he didn't mention the offer of marriage to the gentleman's mother. John hung around for a couple of days, and then decided he should be on his way. He told the gentleman to give plenty of money to the poor, and he took to the road. After a while he arrived back home, but life there bored him, so he thought he would rejoin his regiment. He set out again on his travels, and at last he came to the hill overlooking the town where the regiment was stationed. And who should pop up but Old Clootie.

'Ho John, you've come back.'

'That's right, I have come back,' said John. 'And who are you?'

'I'm Old Clootie. Don't you remember? You gave yourself to me last time you were up here.'

'How do I know who you are? I've never seen you before. There's a queer look about you, right enough, but I don't believe you're telling the truth. You'll have to prove it to me – turn yourself into a snake.'

In a flash Old Clootie was hissing and slithering across the brow of the hill. John told him to turn himself into a lion and, in another flash, a great, maned beast was roaring into his face.

'Throw out fire seven miles in front of you, and seven miles behind.' Old Clootie bent over. A jet of flame seven miles long came out of his mouth, and another out of his rear end.

'I'm convinced,' said John. 'Since I'm to be your servant, climb into my knapsack and I'll carry you. But you mustn't come out until I tell you, otherwise the deal's off.'

Old Clootie agreed and climbed into the knapsack, and John set off back to his regiment but, as soon as he entered the town, people started to call out, 'It's John the deserter!' He was arrested and taken before a court martial, where he was condemned to be hanged at noon the next day. John asked if he could take the bullet instead, and the colonel agreed, as John was an old soldier who had spent so long in the army.

The next day John was taken out to the courtyard, and the soldiers were chatting around him, discussing the execution. 'What are they saying?' growled Old Clootie from inside the knapsack. 'Set me free. I'll soon sort them out.'

The chattering stopped. The colonel and the soldiers were silent. 'What's that in your knapsack?' said the colonel.

'It's just my white mouse.'

'I don't care whether it's black or white, don't open that knapsack. Get out of here now. I'll give you a letter of reprieve, and I don't ever want to see you again.'

So John went away, with the knapsack over his shoulder, and at dusk he came to a barn where there were twelve men threshing. 'Hey boys,' said John. 'Could you do me a favour? I've got this old knapsack and it's so stiff it's taking the skin off my back. Maybe you could beat it with your flails to make it softer.'

The threshers set to for a couple of hours. The knapsack was jumping about all over the place until it became so agitated that it started to knock the men over. They didn't like this at all. 'Get out of here, and take that thing with you,' they told John. So John set off again, with the knapsack over his shoulder, until he came to a forge where there were twelve smiths, their hammers ringing out in the night.

'Hey, lads, how are you? I've got this old knapsack, and it's so stiff it's taking the skin off my back. There's half a crown for each of you, if you give it a good going over with your hammers.'

The smiths thought this was great sport, but with every blow the knapsack leapt up to the roof beams. The smiths became suspicious. 'There's something not right about that knapsack. Get it out of here, and take yourself with it.'

So John left the smithy with Old Clootie on his back, and they came to an ironworks where there was a blazing fiery furnace.

'What's happening now?' Old Clootie whined from inside the knapsack.

'Just be patient, and you'll find out.'

'Let me out,' said Old Clootie. 'I can't take any more. I'll never bother you again in this world.'

'Nor in the next?'

'Nor in the next.'

'Right,' said John, 'we'll stop here for a smoke.' He threw the knapsack into the furnace, the knapsack and Old Clootie went up to the heavens in a great explosion of green flame – and John went on his way.

– The Battle of the Thumbs –

'That's where they were buried, some of them from the battle. It's a place near An Crossan, beyond Scoor; Cille Chaoibein – that's the name of it.' Place-names soon cropped up in any conversation with Johnnie Chalein, as John Campbell was known. This warriors' resting place is not on the map, nor is the meaning of its name now clear; but the mere mention of it led us at once to a grisly affray from 'a long long time ago'.

Much of Johnnie's huge store of Mull tradition was learned at the fireside of Donald Morrison, twenty years his senior. He, in turn, had heard this story from a neighbour born in the early 1800s. With characteristic gusto, voice rising and falling, finger jabbing the air at key moments, Johnnie always concentrated on the final part of the action, played out across the landscape that he himself had worked in as labourer or farmhand – or walked through as a postman – all his life.

But it began as follows. MacGillivray of Glencannel, out hunting in Glen More, was shot dead by a clansman of Maclean of Duart. No one knows why. But the victim had no quarrel with Duart; in fact the two were close. The miscreant fled, to take refuge with MacPhie of Colonsay. Maclean demanded his return, for justice to be meted out, but what came back from Colonsay was the murderer's head with, what's more, a twig poked through the eye-sockets. This insult brought a furious riposte from Maclean, to which the MacPhies' reply was to sharpen their swords and set sail for the south coast of Mull. Johnnie takes up the tale:

Port Bheathain, that's where the Colonsay men came in. The lookouts in the fort, up on Dun a' Gheird there, they saw the boats far off and lit a fire. Others saw it and lit a fire too, so the word went round, all round Mull – they were to meet where the first fire was lit.

A fighting man from Ardtun brought a good number of big men with him, Beatons they were, bowmen – and Oh by God! they were good. They were saying that these Beatons marched over the moor beyond Assapol, just trying out their arrows. And they were shooting the tops of the white bog-cotton clean off!

And when they were all gathered this crafty old fellow told them what to do, he knew how the land lay do you see? 'You're not going straight for the shore,' he said. 'The tide's on the ebb so let them draw up their boats. You stay a bit back, keep to the higher ground.'

Then off he ran. And the signal was that he'd take off his bonnet and they'd see his head – his bald head. At that they jumped up and got between the Colonsay men and the shore. Some of the MacPhies broke through, making for the boats, but these were high and dry now. They were trying to shove them down to the sea when the Mull men attacked again, hacking at the hands on the gunwales.

Oooh … the Macleans won without a doubt. And afterwards they gathered up EIGHT buckets of thumbs! and the survivors, well, they let them go off in their boats all right – but without their thumbs.

From then on, some gave that sandy inlet a different name, Port nan Ordag or The Bay of the Thumbs.

– Conall Yellow Claw –

There was a time when Ireland was divided into five parts, and each part had a king to rule over it. Conall Yellow Claw lived in one of these kingdoms, a man with four boisterous sons. One day the boys got into a fight with the king's sons, and they killed the oldest of them. Conall was brought before the king, who knew him well. 'Conall,' he said, 'how has it come to this, that your boys have killed my eldest son? I should take revenge and hang the lot of them, but I know it wouldn't do me any good. Instead I have a task for you. If you and your sons can fetch me the brown horse of the King of Lochlann – Norway – I'll spare all four.'

'Your majesty,' replied Conall, 'you are my king, and I owe you allegiance. Even if my sons had done nothing wrong I would still obey your command. It's a hard thing you ask, and we may lose our lives attempting it, but we'll do everything in our power to bring back the brown horse.'

Conall went home, terribly troubled by what the king had asked of him. That night, in bed, he told his wife what he had agreed to, and she was dismayed. 'You should have let him do what he wanted with those crazy boys. If you go off on this wild horse chase, I might never see you again.'

Next morning Conall and his four sons were scudding over the waves, but once they reached Lochlann they hadn't a notion what to do next. 'We'll go and find the king's miller,' said Conall. 'The mill is always a good place to find out what's going on.'

The miller was happy to put them up for the night. Conall said that he would pay him if he could help with the quest for the brown horse. The miller listened sympathetically, but he told Conall that the king was as fond of the horse as he was of anything, and that if Conall wanted it, he would have to steal it.

'I have an idea,' said Conall. 'You work for the king all the time. You could hide me and my sons in five of the sacks of the bran that goes to the stables to feed the horses.' The miller agreed, the sacks were delivered to the stables, and the doors locked for the night. When the coast was clear, Conall and his sons climbed out of the sacks and tried to take hold of the horse, but the animal was as good as wild, and the racket it made echoed through every room in the palace.

The king woke. He told his servants to go to the stables and see what was troubling the brown horse. By the time the servants got there, Conall and his sons were hiding in the shadows; so the servants went back to the king and reported that nothing seemed to be amiss.

When they tried a second time to take hold of the brown horse, the noise was even more thunderous. Again the king sent down his servants to the stables, and again they reported back that everything appeared to be in order, because Conall and his sons were once again hiding in dark corners. 'If it happens a third time, I'll go and see for myself,' said the king. And happen again it did, so the king went to the stables with his servants and immediately noticed that there were footprints in the bran that was scattered over the floor. 'There are men hiding in here,' he said to the servants. 'Follow the footprints into the shadows and you'll find them.'

So Conall and his four sons were caught. 'Now Conall,' said the king, for Conall was known far and wide, 'what are you doing here in my stables?'

Conall told the king his story, how he had come to take the brown horse so that he could save the life of his sons. 'Your majesty, I wouldn't have come here if it hadn't been necessary. I confess I was planning to steal the brown horse, for I knew you wouldn't part with it otherwise. Now all I can do is throw myself on your mercy.'

The king told the servants to take the four sons away and give them something to eat, but to make sure that they didn't escape. Then he turned to Conall. 'You're in deep trouble. Tomorrow morning I plan to hang your four sons. But I understand that you were forced into this, so I'll make a bargain with you. If you can tell me of a tighter spot you've been in than the one you're in now, I'll spare your youngest son.'

'Indeed I can tell you of a tighter spot,' said Conall. And this was his story:

'When I was a boy, my father had a lot of land and we had parks full of year-old cattle. One of them had just calved, and my father told me to bring the calf and its mother back home. I took a herd boy to help me and, when we were on our way back with the cow and the calf, we were caught up in a blizzard, so we went into a bothy to shelter until it was over. In the middle of the storm the door opened, and in came a band of eleven cats. A wild bunch

they were, and their ringleader was a great one-eyed brute, with a coat as red as a fox's. I didn't like the look of them at all. "Come on," said the one-eyed monster to the rest of them, "sing a dirge for Conall Yellow Claw."

'I was amazed that they knew my name, and what a caterwauling they made. When they'd finished, the chief bard said, "Now Conall, pay the cat choir for their serenade."

'"I've nothing to give you," I said, "unless you want to take the calf." Immediately they fell on the poor creature, and in seconds there was nothing left but bare bones and a few scraps of hide.

'"Come on boys," said the one-eyed cat, "another ditty for Conall." This time the noise was truly hideous, as if the graves had opened, and the dead were howling a midnight chorus. Again the leader demanded payment.

'"I'm sick of you and your demands," I said. "There's nothing for you unless you want to take the cow." They made short work of the beast, and immediately they struck up singing again, as if the very demons in the pits of hell were calling out for souls to torture. The red-coated cat fixed me with his one eye. "Surely a song as fine as that should be rewarded. Come on, Conall, pay up or it'll be the worse for you." I told them they could have the herd boy. He bolted through the door with the cats after him, while I climbed out of the window and ran off into the forest. I don't know what happened to the boy, but it wasn't long before I heard the cats coming after me, rustling and spitting through the bushes. I found the tallest tree in the forest and climbed to the very top, where the branches were close together and the leaves were thick. The cats were milling around, saying to each other that they didn't know where I was, and they were tired, and they should be getting back home, when the leader suddenly appeared in the midst of them. "I can see more with one eye than the rest of you can with two. Look up, you idiots. There he is in the top of that tree." As soon as they spotted me, one of them began to climb up the tree. When he got close, I took out my knife and sliced off his head. The one-eyed redcoat started to wail. "I can't afford to lose warriors like this. Get round the tree and start digging."

'The cats began to dig and, the first root they severed, the tree gave a shudder and I gave a yell. Not far away a priest was keeping an eye on ten men who were digging a ditch. When he heard me cry out, he said he thought they should go and see if anyone was in difficulty, but the wisest man said they should wait, so they carried on digging. The cats scrabbled furiously in the earth, and a second root gave way. The tree tottered, and I shouted out a second time. "There's a man in trouble," said the priest, but again they told him to hang fire. Then the third root was cut through, and with a terrible creak the tree started to topple slowly. I yelled again, and this time the men came running. I watched as they attacked the cats with their spades, and the cats tore at them with their claws. When the battle was over, not a cat nor a man was left alive.

'And that, great King of Lochlann,' said Conall, 'was when I found myself in an even tighter spot than I am at present.'

'Well, Conall,' said the king, 'you can certainly tell the tale, and you've saved the life of your youngest son, no question about that. I'm thinking now, if you can tell me of even harder circumstances, that would save the life of your third son.'

Conall was sure that he could cap the tale of the murderous cats, and so he began his second story:

'My father's land, which had the great cattle parks, also included a part of the coast that was riddled with caves and coves and stony inlets. One day I was walking along the cliff top, when it seemed as if smoke was rising up out of the ground. In fact, it was coming out of a big pothole. As I peered down the pothole I lost my footing and fell into the darkness, but my fall was broken by a thick bed of dung, and I was quite unharmed. My first thought was how to get out. I looked up and realised it would be impossible to climb out the way I'd entered. Then the ground began to shake, and a huge man came into the cave by an entrance on the shore, driving a herd of goats before him, with a big buck at the head. I saw that the giant was blind in one of his eyes. After he'd tethered the goats he noticed me. "Ho, Conall," he said, "it's been a long time. My knife has been rusting in its sheath waiting to cut a slice out of you."

'"Do as you please," I replied, "though I don't think you'd get more than one meal out of me. But I see that you're blind in one eye. I have some experience as a doctor, and I'm sure I could restore your sight if you'll let me try."

'Of course, he agreed. I told him to fill the cauldron with water and light a fire under it. Then I got some heather and made a scrubber, and told the giant that if I scrubbed his good eye with it, I could magic its sight over to the other. He agreed, and soon the good eye was as blind as the bad one. When the giant realised what had happened he sat himself down in the mouth of the cave and swore that he would have revenge for the loss of his sight. I had to hold my breath all night so that he wouldn't be able to hear where I was.

'At last the sun rose, and the birds began to sing. The giant heard the tweeting, and knew it was day. "Are you awake?" he said to me. "Let the goats loose so they can go outside." I took out my knife and slaughtered the buck. "What are you doing with the goats?" asked the giant, "It sounds as if you're killing my darling, precious buck."

'"Not at all," I replied, "I'm just having trouble untying them."

'I let out one of the goats and the giant caressed her as she passed him. "There you are, you shaggy, hairy creature," he said as tears rolled down his cheeks. "You can see me, but I can't see you." One by one I released the goats, and all the time I was flaying the buck. When the last goat was out of the cave I put on the buck's skin, with my legs in the place of his back legs, my arms in the place of his forelegs, my head in the place of his head, and his horns on top. When I left the cave, the giant stroked my back. "My pretty buck," he said. "You can see me, but I can't see you."

'I was more than pleased to be out of the cave. I shook off the buck's skin and shouted to the giant that I was free, in spite of his efforts. He replied that he wanted to reward my resourcefulness by giving me a gold ring. Of course I didn't trust him, and wasn't going to go anywhere near him, but the gift of the ring was enticing, so I told him to throw it to me. I picked it up and slipped it on my finger, and then the giant called out, "Ring, where are you?"

'"Here I am," replied the ring, and immediately I realised my mistake, for the ring clung tight to my finger and I couldn't get it off. The giant lurched towards me. I had to move quickly. I took out my knife, cut off the finger with the ring on it, and threw it far out to sea. "Ring, where are you?" the giant called again.

'"Here I am," the ring called back, from the depths of the ocean. The giant plunged in and drowned, and that was the end of him. I went back into his cave and gathered together all his treasure; then I went home, and everyone was delighted to see me. And by the way, great King of Lochlann, if you doubt my story, here's the proof.'

And Conall held up a hand that was missing one of its fingers.

'Well Conall,' said the king, 'very impressive, you've done it again. That was indeed a difficult situation, and now you've saved the lives of two of your sons. Would you like to try again? The story of an even harder circumstance will cause me to spare your second eldest son.'

'Indeed, your majesty,' said Conall, 'I think I may have just the tale.' And this is the third tale that Conall told to the King of Lochlann:

'After my father had found me a wife, and I was married, I went on a hunt. I came to a loch, and in the middle of the loch was an island. Close to the shore was a boat and I could see that it was full of precious things. I thought I would go and take them, but no sooner had I stepped into the vessel than it started to move towards the island. It reached the shore and I got out, and the boat drifted back the way it had come. I didn't know what to do. There was no sign of a house or a bothy, or of anything living at all.

'I decided to explore. I climbed a hill and looked down on to a glen, and there, at the bottom of a chasm, was a woman with a naked child on her knee and a knife in her hand. The woman put the knife to the baby's throat, and when the baby laughed in her face she threw the knife behind her. Then she picked up the knife, and the whole rigmarole was repeated.

'It was a strange and dangerous place. "What are you doing here?" I called down to the woman.

'"Who are you?" she shouted back. I told her who I was and how I got there. "That's just what happened to me," she said, and she took me to where she was staying. It was a giant's cave, and the giant had told her that she must kill and cook her own child for him to eat, otherwise that would be the end of her. I started to explore, and soon found a room full of naked corpses. I cut a chunk out of the freshest corpse and tied some string round it; then I put the piece of flesh in the baby's mouth and tied the other end of the string to his toe. He could chew on the flesh, and, if it slipped down his throat and he began to choke, his legs would jerk and the string would pull the meat back into his mouth. I reckoned that would keep him quiet.

'Then I went back to the room full of corpses, dragged the freshest one down to the kitchen, and told the woman to cook it in place of the baby. "The giant will realise what's happened," she said. "He knows how many corpses there are, and he counts them every day." I told her I would take the place of the corpse myself, and so she did as I asked. We stuffed the corpse into the big cauldron, though we couldn't get the lid on. Then the ground began to shake; the giant was coming home. I stripped off my clothes and hid in the room that was full of dead bodies.

'The giant ate the cooked corpse, all the while complaining that it was too tough to be a child. "I did what you told me," said the woman. "You know how many bodies there are in the room. Go up and count them if you don't believe me." He came up to the room and took an inventory, and of course the number was correct, since I was lying there amongst them.

'"One of those bodies looks particularly white and tasty," said the giant. "I'll have a nap, and eat it when I wake up." When he woke he grabbed me by the ankles, dragged me downstairs and tossed me into the cauldron, then popped on the lid. It was so hot I stuck to the bottom, and I thought I would roast in there. After a while the woman put her lips next to the opening and asked if

I was alive. I replied that I was, and she told me the giant had gone back to sleep, so I should climb out of the pot. I got out, leaving behind the skin of my buttocks, but I was at a loss as to what to do next. The woman told me that the only weapon that would kill the giant was his own spear, which was standing in a corner. I managed to manoeuvre it down and began to advance towards him. He was an ugly brute, and I noticed for the first time that he had just one eye in the middle of his forehead. His breathing was so heavy that, as I got closer, I thought I would be sucked into his maw or blown away like a straw in the wind. But I plunged forward and speared him in the eye.

'The giant reared up and struck the end of the spear on the roof of the cave. It went right through the back of his head, and he fell down stone dead.

'And you can be sure, great king of Lochlann,' said Conall, 'that I was never happier in all my life. The woman and I left the cave and slept through the night out in the open. Next morning the boat was waiting to take us and the baby back to dry land, and then I returned home.'

While Conall was telling his third story, the king's mother had been in the room, making up the fire. 'Was that you on the island?' she asked Conall.

'Indeed it was, every word is true.'

'Well I was there too. I was the woman, and the king here, my son, was the baby that you saved from the giant's belly.'

'Oh Conall,' said the King of Lochlann, 'you have indeed come through great hardships. Your sons are saved, and the brown horse is yours, together with a sack full of my finest treasure.'

Next morning Conall was up early, and the queen was up even earlier to see him off. He took the brown horse, and a sack full of silver and gold and jewels, and, together with his four sons, he returned to Ireland. He left the treasure at his own house and delivered the brown horse to the king, and ever after that the two of them were the best of friends.

When Conall got back home, he and his wife threw a party. And what a party it was!

~ THE GIRL AND THE DEAD MAN ~

Ann Darroch told this story to Hector MacLean on Islay in May 1859. She learned it from an old woman, Margaret Conal, of whom MacLean wrote:

> I have some recollection of her myself; she was wont to repeat numerous 'ursgeulan' (tales). Her favourite resorts were the kilns, where people were kiln-drying their corn; and where she was frequently rewarded, for amusing them in this manner, by supplies of meal. She was paralytic; her head shook like an aspen leaf, and whenever she repeated anything that was very exciting, her head shook more rapidly; which impressed children with great awe.

J.F. Campbell recalls hearing that the very same kiln that Margaret Conal 'used to haunt' had, in earlier times, been used for illegally distilling whisky:

> A child would not easily forget a story learned amongst a lot of rough farmers, seated at night around a blazing fire, listening to an old crone with palsied head and hands; and accordingly, I have repeatedly heard that the mill, and the kiln, were the places where my informants learned their tales.

'The Girl and the Dead Man' has some similarities to John MacDonald's 'The Tale of the Soldier'. Here it is now.

There was a poor woman who had three daughters. One day the eldest said to her mother, 'I'm away to seek my fortune.'

The woman set about baking a bannock, for the girl to take with her. When it was cooked, she asked her daughter whether she would like the smaller portion, together with a mother's blessing, or the larger portion together with her curse.

'I'll take the big bit and the curse,' said the girl. She set off and, as night wreathed round her, she sat at the foot of a wall and started to eat the bannock. A crowd of creatures gathered: a collie and her pups, and a flock of birds. They asked the girl if she would share the bannock. 'Certainly not, you ugly lot. There's not enough here for me.' She set off into the darkness and, after a while, there was a light in the distance. She reached the house and knocked on the door, and they asked who she was. 'A good maid looking for a master.'

'Just what we need,' they replied. The girl was offered a bucket of gold and a bucket of silver for her wages. In return she was expected to sleep through the day and then stay awake all night, keeping watch over a dead man. He was the brother of the woman of the house, and he was under a spell.

The girl was given a bed with green silk sheets, and everything she needed to help her stay awake – thimbles, needles and thread, as many candles as she could burn, and as many nuts as she could crack. But the very first night, when she was supposed to be keeping watch, she fell asleep. The mistress came in and hit her on the back of the head with a magic club, and she fell down dead. They took the body and threw it out of the back door, on top of the midden.

Not long after, the middle sister told her mother that she thought she should go and seek her fortune. Things went for her just as they had for the oldest girl: a big bit of bannock and a mother's curse, a stingy refusal to share her food, the task of keeping night watch over the dead man; then falling asleep on the job, the magic club, and a sticky end next to her sister as a cold corpse on the dung heap.

Eventually the youngest girl told her mother that she was off to seek her fortune; but, unlike her sisters, she took the tiny bit of bannock together with her mother's blessing. At nightfall when she was eating, the animals came to ask for food, and she shared the bannock with them. The dogs snuggled up to her, and the birds covered her with their wings to keep her warm.

The girl came to the house with the light, and told them, as her sisters had done before, that she was a good maid looking for a master. They took her in and gave her the job of keeping night watch over the dead man. She sat patiently with a stick at her side, sewing away by candlelight with the needle and thread that had been left for her, and cracking nuts when she felt peckish. Some time around midnight the dead man opened his eyes. Slowly he sat up and grinned at the girl. 'If you don't lie down properly,' she told him, 'I'll give you a good leathering with this stick.'

The dead man lay down again, but it wasn't long before he was up on his elbow a second time, smirking away. 'You'd better listen to me,' said the girl, 'because I won't tell you again. If you don't lie down and stay down, you'll get a taste of this stick.'

Soon after, the dead man was up for a third time with the same daft grin on his face. The girl picked up her stick and whacked him across the shoulder. The stick stuck to the corpse, her hand stuck to the stick, and the dead man leapt up and rushed out of the house. He dashed through the woods, trailing the girl behind him. Under and over the branches they went, blinded by nuts and scraped by thorns, until finally they were back in the house. The dead man threw himself on the bed. The club loosened from his shoulder, the girl's hand loosened from the club, and he was at peace. The spell had been broken.

They gave the girl a bucket of gold and a bucket of silver, together with a magic potion. She went out into the back yard where her two sisters lay side by side on the midden, and brought them back to life by rubbing them with the potion. The three of them went back home to their mother, and they left me sitting here – and if all's well with them, all well and good, and if all's not well, they've only themselves to blame.

The Unbidden Three

Triùir a thig gun iarraidh – Gaol, Eud is Eagal.

The Gaelic proverb says that there are 'three that come unbidden – Love, Jealousy and Fear'. The following stories deal with the vagaries of the human heart, and are shot through with the arrows from those overwhelming emotions that can strike without warning. Coincidentally, two of the stories share the location of Ben Cruachan, where the Cailleach Bheur kept her cow; and, in all three, the central characters undertake journeys that will change the courses of their lives.

It's been suggested that the story of Diarmid and Grainne goes back to the tenth century, though the earliest text is from sixteenth-century Ireland, and keeps the story firmly in that country. The Argyll version, on which this retelling is based, was collected on Islay in 1859. It carries the two lovers across the sea to Kintyre, and ultimately to Ben Cruachan, overlooking Loch Etive. Apart from the lovers themselves, a pivotal character is the legendary Irish warrior-hero Finn MacCool, whose exploits and adventures were once widely popular with storytellers in Highland Scotland.

The story of the Mull Harper became popular around the turn of the eighteenth century. A version appeared in the literary periodical *The Bee* in 1791, Thomas Garnett included it in his *Tour through the Highlands* of 1800, and the Paisley weaver poet Robert Tannahill turned it into a song, 'The Harper o' Mull', which begins:

When Rosie was faithful, how happy was I,
Still gladsome as simmer the time glided by,
I play'd my harp cheery, while fondly I sang,
Of the charms of my Rosie the winter nights lang …

'The Lovers of Callert House' is the most recent story in this group. Intensely romantic as it is, it may have a historical basis.

~ Diarmid and Grainne ~

Finn MacCool had already been married twice, and he was getting old. His first wife had been spirited away under a spell, and his second had died many years before. Now he was preparing to marry King Cormac's daughter Grainne, a beautiful young woman not even half his age.

The wedding feast lasted for seven days and nights, and all Finn's warriors and their wives were there. Among them was Diarmid, an outstanding young man who possessed many skills: as well as being a fine hunter, he was a skilled wood carver, and a champion at board games; and he was second to none for bravery in battle. He had magic in his hands, so that any food he touched came to taste of honey. Diarmid's only weakness was a strange mark on his forehead; if a woman caught sight of it, even for an instant, she fell in love with him. Diarmid was quite shy, and always wore a hat pulled well down, to avoid embarrassing situations.

At the end of the wedding celebrations the dogs were given their own feast. They started to fight over the scraps and bones, and Diarmid waded in to help pull them apart. It was hot work. He lifted his hat to wipe the sweat from his forehead, and Grainne saw the mark, just a glimpse. She came straight up to Diarmid and touched his arm. 'Run away with me,' she said.

'That's impossible.'

'I'm in love with you. You have to take me away from that old man; I want you, not him.'

'I won't take you – not inside or out, clothed or unclothed, on horseback or on foot – and that's an end to it.'

Diarmid was furious, more with himself for his carelessness than with Grainne. He went off to a remote place, built a house and lived there alone. One morning a voice woke him. 'Are you in there, Diarmid?'

'I am. What do you want?'

'I want you to come away with me.'

'Didn't I tell you I wouldn't go with you if you were inside or out, on horseback or on foot, clothed or unclothed?'

'Come and see.'

Diarmid went to the door. Grainne was halfway over the threshold, on the back of a buck goat, and all she wore was a herring net. 'You have to take me now,' she said.

'Finn will hunt us down,' said Diarmid, 'and when he finds us he'll kill me, and probably you as well.'

'We'll put the sea between us and Finn, and we'll hide out in the hills. He'll never find us there.'

Diarmid knew that they must leave. He and Grainne took a boat over to Kintyre and headed inland. As they were crossing a river, Grainne was holding up her skirts to stop them from getting wet. A salmon leapt out of the water right next to her, and slid up the inside of her thigh. 'You're closer to me than Diarmid's ever been,' said Grainne to the salmon.

The runaways found shelter in a place called the Stag's Crag, where they existed like tinkers. Diarmid caught fish and game for them to eat, and he made wooden bowls which Grainne went out to sell. They lived together, but slept apart.

There were wild men in the hills. One of these men, who was known as Crazy Strangerson, found the place where Diarmid and Grainne were staying. He invited himself in and, out of hospitality, they entertained him with a game of dice. Grainne was a young woman, full of passion. With Diarmid denying her any possibility of intimacy, she took a fancy to this new guest. When Diarmid was away working on his bowls, she and Crazy Strangerson cooked up a plot to murder him. Diarmid returned and the wild man pounced. The hero

and Crazy grappled with each other back and forth, until Diarmid finally got the upper hand, but Grainne came up behind him with a knife and stabbed him in the thigh. Diarmid ran off into the hills, hiding out in caves and barely managing to stay alive. His hair and his beard grew long, until they covered the whole of his face.

Grainne and her new lover had been living together at the Stag's Crag for a while when another wild man showed up at the door. This man was carrying a big salmon, and he offered to share it with them if they would let him roast it over their fire. While he was turning the fish, the wild man kept dipping his fingers in a dish of water, as if he was trying to rid them of some kind of smell. When the fish was done, Grainne took a piece and put it in her mouth and it tasted of honey. She knew then that Diarmid was the cook. Crazy Strangerson leapt on Diarmid, and the two wild men wrestled until Diarmid killed Crazy, and ran off into the night.

Next morning, at first light, Grainne went out, following Diarmid's trail. She came to the sea. At the edge of the water a heron was screaming. Grainne looked up and saw Diarmid, far up the slope of a mountain above the shore. She called to him.

'Diarmid, I still love you. Would you eat some bread and meat?'

'I would if I could get them.'

'I've brought them for you, but I don't have a knife.'

'The knife is where you left it, in the sheath. Come up and get it.'

The knife that Grainne had used to stab Diarmid was still in his thigh, waiting for her to take it out.

Diarmid was afraid that Finn would catch up with them, so they headed north till they came to a glen in the shadow of Ben Cruachan. They camped out by the side of the burn, living together but always sleeping apart.

In fact, Finn had given up the search, thinking that Diarmid and Grainne must both be long dead. It was by sheer chance that he and his men came to the shores of Loch Etive, below Ben Cruachan, hunting a notorious wild boar, a gigantic creature whose bristles dripped with poison.

Diarmid was up in the glen, making his bowls, and the burn had carried the wood shavings down to the shore. Finn saw the shavings. 'This is Diarmid's handiwork,' he said. His men told him it wasn't possible, that Diarmid was dead.

'He's alive,' said Finn. 'Make the call to hunt.'

In the glen, beside the burn, Diarmid heard the call to hunt coming up from the loch's shore. 'That's the call of my brothers in arms. I have to reply.'

Grainne pleaded with him not to reply, that it was a trick, but Diarmid made the answering cry and went down to the shore. Some kind of reconciliation must at least have been feigned, because the hunt began in earnest, and it was led by Diarmid. He roused the boar with the poisonous bristles from its lair, and pursued it down the mountain. The great beast turned on him, and there was a savage fight, until Diarmid thrust his sword under its foreleg and into the heart, and the boar dropped.

Secretly, Finn hadn't forgiven Diarmid for stealing his wife, and was hoping for revenge. He told Diarmid to measure the boar by walking along its back. Diarmid paced from head to tail across the smooth carpet of bristles, and announced that it was sixteen feet.

'Are you sure?' said Finn. 'Try again, from tail to snout.'

Diarmid started off back along the boar's spine. One of the bristles went into his heel and he teetered, then he tumbled off the animal's back.

Finn looked at Diarmid. In spite of their estrangement, he felt pity for his old companion. He asked what would cure him.

'A drink of water from Finn's hands would cure me.'

Finn went to the edge of the loch, cupped his hands, and scooped up the water. As he carried it back, to wet Diarmid's lips, he kept thinking of Grainne, and how he had been betrayed. Every time he thought of the betrayal, Finn let a little of the water slip between his fingers. When he got to Diarmid and leant over him, the last drops fell on the ground, and Diarmid died.

Finn and his men climbed up the glen, by the burn which had washed down the shavings from Diarmid's bowls. They found Grainne, and they found the shelter where she and Diarmid had been staying. When Finn saw that there were two sets of bedding, he realised that his friend hadn't betrayed him as he had thought; and he wished, too late, that Diarmid could be brought back from the dead.

~ THE HARPER OF LOCHBUIE ~

Clan chieftains were once great patrons of the arts. They would employ poets, pipers, singers, and clarsairs; the clarsairs in particular – skilled players of the harp – were often figures with an international reputation, who moved from one post to another and were treated more like guests than servants. The tradition eventually went into decline, and the last clan harper played his final *puirt* some time in the early decades of the eighteenth century. This story took place a hundred years or so before then.

Loch Buie is a sea loch on the south side of Mull, sheltering the settlement of Lochbuie at its head. It's much more easily reached by water than overland. The Laird of Lochbuie had a son who was a bright boy and loved playing out of doors. There was a girl, the daughter of a widow who was one of Lochbuie's servants, and she and the boy were always together, running through the woodlands and up the slopes, swimming in the water at the edge of the loch. At evening they would walk along the shore holding hands, and they sometimes talked of getting married, as childhood sweethearts do.

When he was twelve years old, Lochbuie's son was sent to France, to get a gentleman's education. As time passed, the girl grew up to become a beautiful young woman, a trusted servant in Lochbuie's hall. Young men of all classes tried to flirt with her, and some asked her to marry them, but she gave them no attention because she was convinced that young Lochbuie would come back and claim her hand.

Around the time that the girl first began to doubt the inevitability of her loved one's return, Lochbuie decided to employ a harper. This man had worked all over Europe – in Rome, Paris, Dublin, Canterbury, Cologne – playing for kings and princesses, bishops and warlords. When he was a young man the itinerant life had suited him very well. He loved travel, and he loved playing music, and the job brought as much good living as he could cope with. But now he was getting older; travelling tired him, and he was thinking that he should consider settling down, perhaps even getting married. This quiet spot by the loch side on the island of Mull seemed just the place to rest and wonder about these possibilities.

The harper settled happily into his new post. Life dawdled along; there was plenty of fresh game to eat, and the wine was surprisingly good for such a remote location. The blacksmith was able to fashion new harp pins and brass strings if they were needed, and there were skilled joiners to make any small repairs to his clarsach. Unlike some other patrons, Lochbuie seemed to enjoy the music, and even encouraged the harper to create new compositions, something he hadn't done for a long time. What pleased the harper more than anything else was that, whenever he played, he would notice a pretty servant girl listening like a bright bird, with her head cocked to one side, quite plainly enchanted. Experience had taught him how easily music could stir amorous feelings. Sometimes this had got him into trouble – he recalled one early morning when he needed to flee Padua in a hurry – but he foresaw no trouble here, just the smallest possibility that love of the music might grow into affection for the player.

Shy passing words between the harper and the girl became conversations about anything from the patience of the heron, to how a face or a way of walking might inspire a melody. The two of them were often seen out walking together and, though a few cruel words were spoken by gossips, most people were delighted when the marriage was announced, then celebrated with a great feast, and with plenty of music and dancing. The couple set up in a cottage on the estate, and it was plain that they were very happy together. Both continued to work for Lochbuie. The girl was a good cook and kept her husband well fed, the lively conversations continued between them, and every evening, before they went to bed, the old harper would play, while his young wife closed her eyes, and dreamed of all the wonderful things that he had described to her from his travels – the golden, painted palaces, the dancing girls lithe as hinds, the rivers broad as deserts.

They married in the autumn and, the following spring, the harper had been asked by Lochbuie to play at the wedding of a relative who lived in the north of the island. His wife got permission to put aside her duties for a few days and go with her husband, and they set off on a bright morning in early April up Gleann a' Chaiginn Mhòir, the Glen of the Big Rocky Pass. At any time of the year the Highland weather can change abruptly. Around noon on this particular day, which had begun so well, a cold wind blew white cloud in from the west and, as they climbed higher, a few flakes of snow started to fall. By the end of the afternoon, with the light beginning to fade, the harper and his wife were struggling through a blizzard. The girl had set out in the lightest spring clothes, completely unprepared for the return of winter weather, and even her husband's cloak around her shoulders couldn't keep out the cold.

By the time they reached a cave, high up in the mountains, the harper was wondering in desperation how he could make his wife warm. He had the means of making fire, a flint and steel, and some dry moss, but nothing to burn. There were no trees or even bushes growing in the pass, and just a few twigs, brought in by nesting birds, on the floor of the cave. He gathered the twigs together and made a fire beneath them. He unpacked his harp, picked up a stone and began to break up the instrument, then fed the pieces to the fire. The sound box of the harp had been carved out of a single piece of sycamore, and there was soon a good blaze going. The harper and his wife huddled close to the fire, hoping it would keep burning until dawn. They had some bannocks and cheese, which they ate, and then they sat without speaking, looking into the flames.

Late in the night, after hours of staring at the embers of the burnt harp, the girl first, and then the man, heard the sound of a horse's hooves coming through the racket of the wind. The horse halted near the mouth of the cave, the rider dismounted, and a young man came in. He greeted them, and sat down on the other side of the fire. He told them they were unfortunate to be in such a place on a night like this, and how lucky it was that he had a flask with him. The young man handed the brandy to the harper's wife. She took a sip from the silver neck and her eyes sparkled in

the fire's light. The harper himself drank, then handed the brandy back to the young man, but the young man told him to hold on to it. He took a few more sips, and said that it was good brandy, as good as any he had tasted in France.

As the young man and the girl talked quietly, the harper fell asleep. When he opened his eyes there was enough daylight coming into the cave for him to see that the night's fire was now grey ash. He sat up stiffly and looked around; there was no sign of either his wife or the young man. The harper stood and went to the cave's entrance. In the snow he saw two sets of footprints going a short way, a disturbance as their owners mounted the horse, and the hoof prints of the horse itself going back down the pass.

Lochbuie's son had finally returned to claim his childhood sweetheart, and he had found her in a cave high up in the mountains, in a pass which is still called Mam an Tiompain, the Pass of the Harp. The harper turned and looked back at the remains of the fire, and said, '*Is mairg an losg mi an tiompan dhuit.*'

'What a fool I was to burn my harp for you,' is still the proverbial phrase to use when a favour goes unrequited.

~ The Lovers of Callert House ~

Callert House is a small mansion off the north shore of Loch Leven, built by Sir Duncan Cameron of Fassifern around 1835. The building hasn't been lived in for over seventy years, and has fallen into a ruinous state, although it is being slowly restored. To the west are the remains of the previous thatched house, which itself was destroyed by the Duke of Cumberland's troops in the wake of the 1745 uprising.

An even earlier building was burnt down around 1640. Just before the blaze, the laird's daughter, whose name was Mairi, had been at odds with her father. She was a lively and generous young woman who, in his opinion, spent far too much time with the tenants of the estate; so, to punish her, he locked her in her room. While Mairi was imprisoned, a Spanish trading ship moored in Loch Leven, full of beautiful clothes to sell. Apart from Mairi, the whole family from Callert House went down to the ship, together with the servants. When they returned she could hear the voices below, rejoicing in their purchases, and she imagined she could even hear the rustling of the silks and satins. There was one dress so exquisite that all the women tried it on in turn.

Next morning, when Mairi woke, she listened for conversations from around the house, for she was missing human company and hoped that this was the day that she would be set free. But the house was oddly silent and, although she called out, no one answered. The door of her room was stout and locked tight, so she couldn't force it, and it was too high up for her to risk jumping out of the window.

It was a good while before Mairi heard voices; people were talking outside in the forecourt. She went to the window and looked down. Among the group was Donald Cameron of Ballachulish, a good friend of the family. Mairi opened the window and waved to him, and he shouted back. Word was about that the Black Plague was in the house. It had come in on the Spanish ship, hiding among the clothes, and everyone in Callert House who had made contact with the silks and satins was now dead or dying.

He had orders to burn the house down to the ground, together with its occupants.

Mairi managed to persuade Donald Cameron to put off razing the place until a message had been sent to her sweetheart, Diarmid, the son and heir of Campbell of Inverawe. Mairi waited until night time, when Diarmid arrived. He threw up a rope for her to climb down, but before they embraced he insisted that she wash in the burn and put on the fresh clothes that he had brought. And as soon as Mairi was out of Callert House, it was put to the flames.

By the time Mairi and Diarmid reached Loch Awe, news of the plague was already there. Old Campbell, Donald's father, shouted down from an upstairs window that he wouldn't let the couple in the house. They would have to spend a month in a secluded bothy on the slopes of Ben Cruachan, to make sure they were free of infection; and he made them take their marriage vows before they left.

After a month in the wild, the young couple returned fit and happy to Diarmid's family, and were welcomed in. Sadly, their happiness only lasted a short while, as Diarmid was killed at the Battle of Inverlochy, in 1645, when Montrose routed the forces of

the Marquess of Argyll. He was buried in the Campbell graveyard by Ardchattan Priory. Later, Mairi was married again, to the Prior of Ardchattan. During a thunderstorm, when they were on their way to Islay, she and her party sheltered beneath a cliff, and were overwhelmed by a fall of rock.

A belief grew up that, when the old Callert House was burnt down, a good quantity of silver and coins had been buried under the ruins. People were scared to dig them up, because they were afraid the plague might still lurk beneath the soil; but, in the nineteenth century, Campbell of Monzie gathered together a band of workmen to excavate the site. On the first day they dug a trench, and found nothing. Next morning, to the workmen's surprise, Monzie ordered them to fill in the trench. No one could understand why – Monzie had nothing to say on the matter – and so the treasure, if treasure there be, still lies buried there.

The Sense They Were Born With

One of the great strengths of folk tales lies in their narrative impetus – how the stories bowl along. The best storytellers, working eyeball to eyeball with a live audience, are able to give just the right amount of information, and no more; they allow enough space for each listener to create his or her own individual version of the story in the great cinema of the imagination.

As a result of this sparseness of detail, which is an essential part of the folk tale's nature, character is generally presented without much subtlety. Kings are old, witches evil, and giants slow-witted. The king's sons, who are the typical heroes of long quest stories like 'The Brown Bear of the Green Glen', are short of worldly experience. Sometimes they are innocent specifically so they can learn to be resourceful. In other cases they learn little, but they get help from both the human and the supernatural worlds; and so, at the end of the story, they land on their feet.

There are some tales, however, whose central theme is the sheer obtuseness of their main characters. In the following three stories a lack of perspicacity – sometimes extreme – leads to circumstances that are, in turn, tragic, farcical, and unexpectedly idyllic.

The Water Horse, which appears in the story of the Big Lad, as well as in the Islay tale in the chapter following, is a sinister creature which lives in many of the lochs and lochans throughout the Highlands. It's often found on the shore, a beautiful animal which tempts the unwary admirer to climb up on its back. But woe to anyone who does so, as the horse immediately plunges into the water and its rider disappears forever – except perhaps for a heart or liver which is found floating on the loch's surface the following morning. The Water Horse's generally more benign cousin is the Water Bull.

~ The Sixty Fools of Achabheann ~

The son of Callum Colgainn had twelve sons of his own, and they were fine, handsome boys. But they began to get sick and to die, one after the other, until there were only two of them left. When they went to seek advice as to what they should do, they were told that each should take a horse, laden with baskets of possessions, and set off in the opposite direction to his brother. Wherever the strap of a basket broke, they should put down and make a home there.

One of the brothers went north and the other south. When the one who was going north was passing through Glen Etive a strap broke, and the basket fell off the horse. He decided that this would be a good place to stay, so he built a house, married and had children, and their descendants became the MacCallums of Glen Etive. The second brother went south, heading for Kintyre. He got as far as Knapdale when one of the baskets fell off his horse, so that was where he made his home. And his descendants became the MacCallums of Knapdale.

Many years passed. The two growing families kept in touch and exchanged news, and each family frequently sent messages to the other to say how much they would like to meet their relatives. Late one year, the MacCallums of Glen Etive sent word to invite the MacCallums of Knapdale to visit them, saying that they would be given the best hospitality. It was either by coincidence or by fate that, at exactly the same time, the MacCallums of Knapdale sent a similar message to the MacCallums of Glen Etive.

Without even waiting to reply to the respective invitations, the men of each family – patriarch, sons and grandsons – set off to visit the house of the other. The two bands met on the range of hills between Craignish and Melfort, on either side of a ford, at a place called Achabheann. It was dusk, and they didn't recognise each other. There were thirty of them on either side, all strong, proud men; too proud to ask who the other party might be, and too proud to step aside and let them pass. Instead they decided to clear a passage with their swords. The slaughter kept on until the waters of the burn ran red, and there were only two left alive. On one side was a young lad, and on the other an older man. Both were exhausted. The older man, who was the less hot-tempered of the two, said that, before they did anything else, they should bury the dead. The younger agreed, and they set to.

When they had finished the burying the younger man challenged the older to continue fighting.

'Since there are only us two left,' said the older man, 'we should at least say who we are, and what our business is.'

'I agree. Tell me what people you belong to.'

'I am descended from the son of Callum Colgainn.'

'I am also descended from the son of Callum Colgainn.'

'Of all the MacCallums of Glen Etive, I am the only one left alive. We were going on a visit to see our relatives in Knapdale, our cousins. Instead we got into a fight, and you and I are the only ones left standing.'

'I am last of the Knapdale MacCallums. We were going to visit our relatives in Glen Etive to enjoy their hospitality. Instead we met here, and have managed to massacre each other.'

'In which case,' said the older man, 'I ask you to kill me. I'd rather be dead than alive.'

But the younger man's temper had cooled, and he wouldn't kill the elder. The older man proposed fighting again, and even suggested that the younger man was afraid, but the goading had no effect. 'Then I will sleep here along with my family,' said the older man, and stabbed himself through the heart with his own dirk.

The last of the Knapdale MacCallums went away and settled in a place which people called 'the little coward's farm'. He married and had children, and his descendants were known as 'the Tribe of the Sixty Fools of Achabheann'.

~ Lochbuie's Two Herdsmen ~

In 1602 the Laird of Lochbuie kept two herdsmen. The wife of one went to pay a visit to the wife of the other, and when she arrived at the house there was a pot bubbling over the fire.

'What have you got in the pot?' she asked.

'A drop of *brochan* – porridge – for my husband to have with his dinner when he comes in.'

'What kind of porridge is it?'

The woman answered that it was *dubh-brochan* – black porridge – which was so thin it was more of a drink than anything else.

'The poor man. You can do better than that. In all the time we've been under the laird, we've never had *brochan* without a bit of beef or something similar in it. The laird would never miss an ox. I'll send my husband over tonight, and he can go with yours and fetch one home for you.'

That evening she sent her husband over to the other woman's house. 'I'll wait for you in the woods,' he said to her man. 'You can go to the fold and steal an ox, and then I'll fetch it back here. No one will know. I'll say I didn't steal it, and you can say you didn't bring it back. We'll both be telling the truth.'

So away they went, into the woods, where they built a fire of peats. The one was to stay by the fire and wait, while the other went off to fetch the ox.

Back in those days, if a man committed a crime he could be hanged without trial or jury, and it happened that Lochbuie had just that day hanged a wrongdoer in the forest near the place where the two herdsmen had their fire.

That same evening, a party of gentlemen had gathered in Lochbuie's castle, and they began to wager with the laird that none of his followers would have the courage to go into the woods and bring back the shoe of the hanged man. Lochbuie put his money down, and called MacFadyen, his big lad, telling him that the winning of the wager depended on him.

MacFadyen said he would go and bring back the shoe but, when he got close to the spot where the hanging had taken place, he saw what he took to be the dead man warming his hands by a fire. He went back to Lochbuie's mansion a lot quicker than he came. When they asked about the shoe, MacFadyen said that, as its owner was out in the woods sitting by a fire, he had left the shoe where it was, on the dead man's foot.

The gentlemen were delighted. 'There you go, Lochbuie, we knew you only kept cowards here.'

There was a crippled man in the room who had lost the use of his legs, and got about on all fours on boards. He reprimanded MacFadyen for losing the wager on behalf of Lochbuie. 'If I had the use of my feet, I would bring back his leg as well as the shoe.'

'Come on then,' said MacFadyen, 'I'll put a pair of legs under you like you've never known.' He swung the crippled man up on to his shoulders, and set off back to the woods.

When they came in sight of the man who was warming himself by the fire, the crippled man begged to go back, but MacFadyen said they would keep going. The man at the fire raised his head and saw them coming. He thought it was his accomplice, with the ox on his back. 'Is that you?' he asked.

'Yes,' MacFadyen replied, 'it's me.'

'Have you brought him?'

'Yes, I have.'

'And is he fat?'

'Fat or thin, you can have him,' said MacFadyen, and pitched the crippled man on to the fire.

MacFadyen ran faster than he'd ever run in his life, with the crippled man close behind him on his four boards. The man at the fire thought he'd been rumbled and that the game was up, so he followed the other two, hoping to make his excuses to the Laird of Lochbuie, while the crippled man looked back, and was convinced he was being chased by the hanged man.

MacFadyen reached the castle first. When they asked him if he had the shoe, he said no. He said the corpse had asked if the crippled man was fat, so the poor creature would surely have been eaten up by now. At that moment the crippled man arrived at the door, and shouted out that the dead man was close behind him. They let him in and, as soon as the door was closed, the herdsman beat on it, and demanded entrance. Lochbuie refused, as he, and everyone else there, thought this was the man they had hanged earlier in the day.

'I'm your own herdsman,' shouted the herdsman, so they opened the door. When he was inside, he explained to them the plan to steal the ox, and how he thought MacFadyen was his companion returning. That was why he'd asked if he was fat; he'd meant the ox, not the crippled man. Lochbuie and the rest found this tremendously amusing, and kept the herdsman there repeating the story until late into the night.

The man who went to steal the ox went back to the spot where he had arranged to meet the other herdsman, but he could find no one. He wandered around in the darkness until he bumped into the corpse dangling from the tree.

'Oh mercy,' he said, 'they caught you and hanged you already. I'll get the same treatment tomorrow night, all because we let women persuade us into this stupid scheme.' He went over to the tree and took down the dead man, without looking at his face. Leaving the ox in the clearing, the herdsman carried the body on his back, up hill and down, through mud and mire, until he arrived at the other herdsman's house. He dumped the corpse in the garden and knocked at the door. The wife let him in, and asked how they'd got on.

'Never mind how we got on, he's been hanged since we went out.'

The woman began to weep and moan. 'Hush,' said the herdsman. 'Keep quiet and don't say a word, or we'll both be hanged tomorrow. We'll bury him in the garden, and no one will ever know. Maybe they'll forget the whole thing.' So they buried the corpse, and the herdsman went home to his wife.

Meanwhile, the herdsman who had been at the mansion thought he should be getting back home himself, as it was late. When he arrived there, he knocked on the door. His wife didn't say a word.

'Let me in, it's me. I've returned.'

'I will not let you in. You've been hanged, and we buried you in the garden. You'll never get in here.'

'What do you mean? I haven't been hanged.'

'I don't care; you're still not coming in.'

He thought the best thing would be to go to the house of the other herdsman, and try to find out what was going on. When he got there he called to his pal to let him in.

'I won't let you in. I had enough carrying you on my back after you'd been hanged.'

He went round to the big window at the end of the house. 'Look, here I am,' he said. 'Get a light, and you'll see that I haven't been hanged, any more than you have.' When the other herdsman realised that this was the truth, he took his friend in, and they were up until dawn, each explaining to the other what had happened from his own point of view. They decided to go to Lochbuie and make a clean breast of it. Lochbuie listened to the story, and there wasn't a year after that when he didn't give them both an ox and a boll of meal.

~ THE SON OF THE STRONG MAN OF THE WOOD ~

There was a big man, known as the Strong Man of the Wood, who spent his days hunting deer and cutting down trees. He had his eye on a large oak but, when he went to cut it down, he miscalculated, and the tree fell on top of him. He was badly hurt, but managed to drag himself from under the tree. When he was on his feet he carried it back home on his shoulders, but he collapsed as soon as he got to the door.

His pregnant wife came out and saw that he was in a bad way, so she got him to bed. As he lay there, the Strong Man of the Wood let out a huge sigh, and said that he was done for. He opened his clenched fist and, in the palm of his hand, there was an acorn. He looked at the acorn, and gave it to his wife. 'I'm going to die,' he said, 'but I want you to plant this acorn by the midden in front of the house. The baby you're carrying, it will be a boy. On the night when he's born, the first shoot from the acorn will peep out of the earth. You must breastfeed our son until he's strong enough to pull up the tree that grows from the acorn by its roots.' These were the last words spoken by the Strong Man of the Wood.

When her time came, the widow gave birth to a son. She asked the midwife to go out into the yard and see if there was a seedling growing from the acorn, and the woman returned to say that there was. The widow breast-fed the boy for seven years. Then she took him out in the yard, and told him to try and uproot the tree. He pushed and he tugged, and he gave the oak a good kicking, but he couldn't shift it. His mother fed him for another seven years. Again she took him out so he could try to pull up the tree, and again, in spite of all his heaving and grunting, he couldn't make it budge.

For yet another seven years the boy thrived on his mother's milk. At the end of that time, out in the yard, he surveyed the oak with narrowed eyes, leapt upon it, tore it out of the ground, chopped it up into firewood with his bare hands, and stacked the wood by the door ready for the winter.

The Big Lad's mother was relieved. 'You've been long enough sucking my breast's sap,' she said. 'Now it's time for you to seek your fortune. Come inside. I'll bake you a bannock, and then off you go.'

The Big Lad got his bannock, and set off down the road to see what he could find in the way of a job. He came to a big estate surrounded by more corn stacks than he had ever seen. He knocked on the door and asked to see the Master, thinking that he might get employment there. The Master came out and asked what he wanted, and the Big Lad said he needed work.

'I don't see why not – you certainly look strong enough. Can you thresh?'

'I certainly can.'

'Well, you'll be tired after your journey. Have a wander round the town, see what's happening on the estate, and you can start work in the morning. There's as much corn in the barn as will keep two men threshing at full pace for six weeks. When you've done that, there's a big yard full of corn stacks behind the barn, and every straw needs to be threshed.'

After he'd had a bite to eat, the Big Lad went to the barn to check out the threshers there. He stood looking at them for a while, and then he took hold of one of their flails. 'I don't think much of this,' he said. 'Wait till you see what I bring with me when I start work tomorrow.' He went out into the wood to cut a flail for himself. When he'd finished, the handle looked more like the mast of a ship than the handle of a flail.

It was a rule of the estate that work should go on from star-set to star-rise. The Big Lad was up early, when the last star was still in the sky. He laid the hay that was housed on the floor of the barn. As he worked his way through, from one end to the other, the roof of the barn rattled and banged and flew up into the air, and by breakfast time there wasn't a single straw that hadn't been threshed. After breakfast, the Big Lad went out into the yard and started to carry the stacks out into the barn, one under each arm, with a third held between his hands. By dinner time the work was done. The barn was up to the beams with grain, and the whole town was white with the straw.

The Big Lad went to find the Master, to ask what he should do next. The Master was wondering why everything was covered with straw, though he didn't mention this to the Big Lad. 'Go and thresh in the barn,' he said.

'I can't. There's nothing left to do there.'

'What do you mean? There's enough work to keep two men busy for six weeks.'

'It's all done. There isn't a straw that hasn't been threshed.'

The Master told the Big Lad to go and get something to eat, and then he went to the barn to find out what had been going on. When he saw that the roof was off, and every straw threshed, he became very scared. He was even more terrified when he saw the size of the Big Lad's flail that was leaning up against the barn wall.

The Master snuck back home, taking one of the narrow lanes to avoid meeting the Big Lad, but the Big Lad spotted him and made straight for him. 'What should I do now?'

'You've done so well today, I think you should rest this evening.'

'Well, you've seen my work now, and you know how good I am, so I'm thinking I should be fed more.' The Big Lad asked for huge amounts, a quarter of a chalder of meal in brose one day, and a quarter of a chalder in bannocks the next, together with the carcase of a two-year-old ox.

'You'll get it,' said the Master, through rattling teeth. He went inside to make arrangements for the feeding, then he asked his advisors to put their heads together and come up with a solution to the problem of the Big Lad, who was going to ruin the place with his appetite. There was a very ancient man called Big Angus of the Rocks, and everyone said they should ask him, for if Big Angus didn't have an answer, no one would.

When Big Angus was told the story of the Big Lad, he wrung his hands and rolled his eyeballs in despair. 'Oh misery and woe! At last he's come! When my grandfather was the age that I am now, and I was just a little boy, I recall him predicting that this place would be laid waste by a huge man, and there's no doubt that your Big Lad is the giant he spoke of. I can only think of one way to get rid of him. Tell him to dig a well out in the field, right down to the water level. It's sandy soil, and he'll have a good way to go. When he's deep down, wait until he bends over, and get your men to shovel the earth back on top of him as fast as they can. But whatever you do, don't let him see what you're up to, or he'll kill the lot of you.'

That night the Master told the Big Lad that a well needed digging, and at first light the Lad set to. The men and the Master went down to see how he was getting on in his hole, and found that he was already so deep that there was a great pile of earth thrown up, and they could only just see the top of his head. They thought they might have missed their chance, but, when they peeped into the hole, the Big Lad was bent over, still digging away. The Master told his men to start shovelling, and they went at it as hard as they could, but the Big Lad stood up, waving his arms, and shouting, 'Go on, get away with you!'

The men scattered, and the Big Lad kept on digging. When the well was finished he went to the Master's house and knocked on the door. There was no reply so he tried the handle. The door was barred, but he gave it a push and the bar broke. Inside he found the Master, crouching under the table. The Master emerged, and asked the Big Lad if he'd finished the well.

'The well's finished, no problem. But why didn't you send a man to keep the rooks away? They were all over me, the pests. Nearly put my eyes out, scratching for worms. Anyway, what would you like me to do next?'

The Master sent for the old man, Big Angus, and told him that his plan hadn't worked.

'We'll have to try again,' said Big Angus. 'Send him up to plough the Crooked Ridge of the Field of the Dark Lake. With luck he'll still be at it when night falls. That's when the Water Horse comes out of the Dark Lake, and nobody has survived an encounter with that beast.'

The Master sent for the Big Lad and told him to go out the next day and plough the Crooked Ridge. Early next morning he set off with his two horses and the plough over his shoulder. He got to the Field of the Dark Lake, yoked the horses, took sight on a large tree that was in the middle of the ridge, and started to plough. Things were going well until the end of the day, when there was a splash from the Lake, and the Big Lad saw a great lump of a thing rearing up out of the water. He ignored it, and carried on ploughing but, when the sun went down, the Thing came out of the lake and hauled itself up to the far end of the Crooked Ridge. Then

it turned round and started to walk towards the Big Lad's team, in the very furrow that he was ploughing. The Big Lad kept going, and met the Thing in the middle of the ridge, close to the large tree. He shouted to it to keep back or take the consequences, but the Thing didn't pay any attention. Instead it opened its mouth and swallowed one of the horses in a single gulp.

'Stop that immediately,' said the Big Lad. 'I'll make you bring that horse back up as quickly as you swallowed him.' He let go of the plough and started to wrestle with the Thing. It was hard going, but at last the Big Lad got the upper hand. 'Put the horse out right now,' he said, but the Thing wouldn't listen.

'I've asked you politely. Now you have no choice.' The Big Lad grabbed the Thing by the tail. He ripped the tree up by its roots, and laid into the Thing until there was nothing left of the tree but a handful of twigs and leaves.

'Now will you put out the horse?' said the Big Lad, but the Thing still refused to obey. 'In that case, you can do the work of the beast that you've eaten.'

The other horse had broken free and run home in terror. When it turned up at the farm, the Master was much relieved. 'Surely that's the end of the Big Lad. The Water Horse of the Dark Lake must have eaten him, and the other horse as well.'

Meanwhile the Big Lad had yoked up the Thing and started ploughing with it, and he didn't finish until every furrow on the Crooked Ridge was turned over. Then he went back to the estate, leading the Water Horse by the head. He came to the Master's door and called to him. No one answered because they were all hiding, so the Big Lad thumped on the door until at last the Master opened it, trembling with fear. The Big Lad asked what his job would be the next day.

'Carry on with the ploughing.'

'There isn't any ploughing to do.'

'The Crooked Ridge should keep two horses going for six weeks.'

'I finished the job.'

'You didn't happen to see anything unusual while you were working?'

'Oh, some big, ugly beast came out of the lake and ate one of the horses. I tried to make it fetch the horse up, but it wouldn't, so I yoked it up and finished ploughing the Crooked Ridge.'

'And what became of the beast?' asked the Master.

'It's here,' replied the Big Lad, and hauled the monster out of the shadows by the scruff of its neck.

'Get rid of it! Make it go away!' the Master screamed.

'Not until it gives up that horse.' The Big Lad wrestled the Thing over on to its back. He took out his knife and slit open its belly, and the horse stepped out alive and well.

'I don't know what to do with the body,' said the Big Lad. 'Best idea is probably to put it down that hole I dug for you. If there's no water there now, there soon will be.' He dragged the beast out into the field and threw it into the well and, when it hit the bottom, it gave a gurgle and became a muddy puddle.

The Master sent for Big Angus of the Rocks. 'What's the news?' asked Big Angus.

'Not good.' The Master told him what had happened – the swallowing of the horse, the yoking up of the beast, the job finished, and the beast destroyed. All that was left was to vacate the estate, and leave the Big Lad to get on with it.

'There's one more thing we could try,' said Big Angus. 'Tell him that you've run out of meal, and that there'll be nothing more for him to eat until he takes some corn to the Mill of Leckan to get it ground. Tell him to hurry, and that he'll need to work all night to get the meal back here first thing in the morning. There's a big lunk of a Brownie in the mill, and no one who tries to spend the night there ever lives to see the dawn. If that doesn't work, you may as well run away and leave him here to his own devices. Whatever you try, he'll ruin the place.'

The Master sent for the Big Lad and told him they were out of meal. He was to fetch the sled, load it up with corn, and take it to the mill, and he would need to work all night to get it ground.

The Big Lad set off. It was dusk when he got to the mill. Everything was dark, as the Miller had finished grinding for the day. The Big Lad went to the Miller's house, and shouted to him to open up the mill. The Master of the big estate had sent him with corn to be ground, and it needed to be done in a hurry.

'I don't care who you are or who sent you,' the Miller shouted back. 'I'm not going to open up that mill for anybody.'

'Give me the key, then. I'll do the job myself.'

'Please yourself. But if you go in there, you won't last the night. The Brownie will see to that.'

The Miller handed over the key, and off went the Big Lad to the mill. He fired up the kiln, dried the corn, and put it in the hopper. Then he got the mill going and ground as much of the corn as he had dried. He riddled the meal and started to make bannocks, as he was starving. While the bannocks were baking on the kiln, a hairy hand stretched out from the shadows and grabbed one of them.

'Stop that,' said the Big Lad, but the Brownie paid no attention. It wasn't long before the hairy hand reached out again, and grabbed another bannock.

'Do that one more time, and you'll regret it,' said the Big Lad, but a third bannock was soon snatched away. 'Since you won't do as I ask, you'll do as you're told. I'll have those three bannocks back, whether you like it or not.'

The Big Lad jumped into the shadows, and landed on top of the Brownie. There was a terrible fight as they threw each other back and forth. The kiln collapsed, the mill was destroyed, and the noise of the battle woke people for miles around. The Miller heard the racket. He was so scared he wrapped himself in the blankets and huddled down at the bed's foot, while his wife shrieked, skittered across the floor, and ended up crouched under the bed.

Finally the Big Lad got the better of the Brownie. 'Please let me go. I'm only a poor old Brownie,' the Brownie begged.

'You can't go free until you rebuild the mill, get the kiln back together, and put the bannocks back on the kiln where you found them.' The Big Lad gave the Brownie a couple of hard thumps, to reinforce the message.

'Let me go,' said the Brownie, 'and I'll do everything you ask.'

'I won't let you go until you do as you're told.'

The Brownie set to work, and it wasn't long before the mill and the kiln were back in working order. But the Big Lad noticed that something was missing. He gave the Brownie a couple more thumps.

'What happened to the bannocks you stole?'

'Please let me go. I'm only a poor old Brownie. You'll find the bannocks in the fireplace.'

'You're not going free until I get those bannocks back.'

The Brownie led the Big Lad to the fireplace, retrieved the bannocks and set them back on the kiln. The Big Lad gave the Brownie a few more thumps for his trouble.

'Let me go,' the Brownie shrieked. 'I'll leave the mill, and I promise I'll never return.'

'I'll take your word for it,' said the Big Lad. He shoved the Brownie through the door, and gave him a kick up the backside into the bargain. The Brownie let out three horrible screams and ran off into the night. The miller heard the screams. Under the bed, his wife wept.

The Big Lad ate the bannocks, then dried and ground the rest of the grain. He riddled the meal, put it in the sacks and put the sacks on the sled. Then he locked up the mill and went back to the Miller's house with the key. The Big Lad shouted, but there was no answer. He shouted again, and a tiny voice answered. The Big Lad said to open the door, as he had the key to the mill.

'Go away! Go away! Take the key with you!' When no one came to the door, the Big Lad gave it a shove and stepped inside.

'It's me. I've ground the meal, and I'm going home. Here's your key.'

When the Miller heard that the grain had been ground, he peeped out from under the blankets. 'You spent the night in the mill, and you're still alive!'

'Pooh! You can spend as long as you like in the mill now. I got rid of the thing that lived there, and it'll never bother you again.'

'Do you hear that, wife?' called the Miller.

'Where is she?' asked the Big Lad.

'She's hiding under the bed. She was terrified by the racket from the mill.'

The Big Lad looked under the bed. He saw a pair of feet. He grabbed the Miller's wife by the ankles and hauled her out, but she was stiff as a board, dead of shock.

The Big Lad gave the key to the Miller and set off back home. There was a brae above the mill which slowed the horse down. The Big Lad gave him a slap on the shoulder to speed him up, but the blow was so heavy it broke the horse's back, and he dropped dead in the road. 'Shame, but never mind,' said the Big Lad. He threw the horse's carcase on the sled, on top of the sacks of meal, and took up the traces himself. In good spirits, he drew the sled to the top of the hill.

The Master wasn't taking any chances. He had lookouts planted on every road that the Big Lad might take to get back to the estate. At last one of the lookouts spotted the Big Lad in the distance, dragging the sled behind him. The lookout threw off his shoes, and every stitch of clothing that might slow him down, and hot-footed it back to the Master's house. 'I've seen him. He wouldn't wait for the horse. He's pulling the sled himself, and he's heading this way!'

'The game's up,' said the Master. 'Everyone out of here, otherwise he'll kill the lot of us.' And they all fled.

The Big Lad arrived back home. He took the horse off the sled, unloaded the sacks of meal, and went to look for company. He searched every nook and cranny, but couldn't find a soul. Finally it dawned on him that he had the estate to himself.

The Big Lad thought this would be a good place to bring his mother, so he went back home and there she was, still in the cottage in the middle of the oak woods. She told him she was too old to walk all that way. 'You carried me for long enough,' he said. 'It's not so far for me to carry you.' He lifted her up on his back and took her to the estate that he'd got for himself, and if they're alive I expect they'll still be there.

Bold Girls

If they are not champions or heroes, the young men in these tales tend to be innocents to the last. They drift through their adventures, buffeted by circumstance and, if they are in a tight spot, it's likely that help will come out of the blue, often from a creature with supernatural powers.

The girls are more resourceful, much better equipped to take charge of their own destinies. Here are three very different stories about bold girls. The first is a local legend from a time when the forests and caves of southern Argyll gave shelter to runaways and wrongdoers of all descriptions. The heroine of 'The Islay Water Horse' employs a trick that Odysseus used three thousand years earlier in his encounter with the Cyclops. 'The Chest', with its Shakespearean cross-dressing, is also a reminder that, although wife-selling was never widespread in Scotland, a woman called Mary Mackintosh was sold by her husband in Edinburgh's Grassmarket in 1828.

~ Home From the Fair ~

The woodlands to the south of Ardrishaig, by Maol Dubh Point, were once infested with robbers. A little girl from there had been with friends to the annual fair, the cattle market, in Tarbert, where she had bought some cakes and, among other trinkets, a penknife. In the evening, on her way back home, she wandered off the path and away from her friends, and came upon a band of men who were robbing the body of a pedlar whom they had murdered. The men looked up and saw the girl, who was so scared that she was unable to move or call out. They grabbed her and took her away to their hut in the middle of the forest. Then they tied her to the body of the pedlar and went away in search of another victim. The girl may have been terrified, but she hadn't lost her wits. She managed to take hold of the little knife she'd bought at the fair, and cut through the rope that bound her to the corpse. When she was free, the girl set off into the dark forest, with no idea of where she was heading.

The robbers returned to their shelter. When they found no sign of the girl, they sent a big dog after her. By this time, she was hiding in a cave a good way away, but the dog followed her scent and tracked her down. It snuffled into the cave and started to growl, so the girl fed it the cakes she'd bought at the fair. When the robbers called from a distance the dog happily went back to them, and they assumed it had been unable to find its prey. At first light the girl got back to the track and found her way home.

– The Islay Water Horse –

The Rinns of Islay lighthouse was built by Robert Stevenson in 1825. It's on the little island of Orsay to the west of Islay, just off the Rinns peninsula. Before there was a lighthouse on Orsay, the island was used for grazing cattle, and a man and a girl had the job of tending to the beasts. One day the man went over to the mainland, and a wild storm rose up which prevented him from getting back, so the girl was left there alone. She was sitting in their hut, warming herself by the peat fire, when the place was surrounded with strange voices. She knew it couldn't be the man who had returned. She looked out of the window, thinking it might be the cattle making the racket, and a big, round pair of eyes looked back at her out of the stormy night. The door opened, and, with a whinnying laugh, the owner of the eyes entered. He was tall and broad, rough and hairy, and his face was skinless and raw.

The stranger lumbered towards the fire, and asked the girl her name. '*Mise mi Fhin*', she told him. 'Me myself.' The thing grabbed hold of the girl. She picked up a ladle full of boiling water and threw it over him, and he ran off shrieking into the darkness. The girl heard a hubbub of unearthly voices asking what was the matter and who had hurt him. '*Mise mi Fhin, Mise mi Fhin*!' – 'Me myself, me myself!' – cried the monster, and his companions let out a howl of mocking laughter. When the laughter died down, the girl ran outside into the storm. She turned loose one of the cows, and then she took a stick, made a circle around herself, and lay down inside the circle. When morning came she was safe, but the cow was dead.

THE CHEST

There was an old king who was keen to see his son married, so he gave the lad fifty pounds, and told him to go out and find himself a wife. The king's son set off, and by nightfall he'd reached an inn. After a hearty meal in front of a roaring fire, he told the innkeeper of his mission. The innkeeper said he need go no further. 'Look out of your bedroom window tomorrow morning, into the little house across the way. The man who lives there has three good-looking daughters, and you'll see them one after the other coming in to get dressed. There've been lots of men who wanted to marry them, but their father insists that the suitors say how old the one they've chosen is, compared with the other two. This is pretty much impossible, as all three of them look alike, but I can tell you that the eldest daughter has a mole on her cheek. A hundred pounds to the old man, and she's yours.'

'I've only got fifty,' said the king's son.

'I'll lend you the other fifty, on condition that you pay me back within a year and a day. Mind, if you renege on the deal I'll have a strip of skin off your back, from the top of your head to the sole of your foot.'

Next morning the king's son watched the girls getting dressed. He thought they were all very beautiful, but he particularly liked the one with the mole on her cheek. After breakfast he went across the road, and they invited him into the sitting room. He told the girls' father that he was looking for a wife, and that he'd heard the man had three fine daughters.

'I do indeed, but I doubt you'll get to marry any of them.'

'I could at least have a look at them.'

The girls were brought in. The father asked the king's son to choose one, and to say whether she was older or younger. He chose the one with the mole, knowing she was the oldest, and asked what her price was. Her father told him a hundred pounds, so he bought her and took her back to his father's house, where they got married.

Not long after the wedding the old king died. A couple of days later the young king was out hunting, when he saw a big ship coming in to the shore. He went down to have a word with the captain and to find out what was on board, and the captain replied that he had a hold full of the finest silk. The king asked for a gown made from the very best.

'You must have a special wife for her to deserve a garment like that,' said the captain.

'Indeed I have. We're not long married, and I can tell you that it would be hard to find her equal for beauty or fidelity anywhere.'

'I'm sure you're right. All the same, I'm a man who likes a wager, however high the odds against me. I'll bet you that I can spend the night in her bedroom, however virtuous you say she is.'

'I'll wager anything you like that you can't,' said the king. The captain staked his cargo of silks, and the king his house and lands. The king remained on board the ship, and the captain went ashore.

The captain knew well enough where the power lay in a royal household. He went straight to the hen-wife, who knew everyone's goings-on, and asked if she could help him get into the queen's bedroom that evening. The old woman told him she didn't think it would be possible but, just as he was about to leave, she grabbed his wrist. 'I've got it! I'm on good terms with the queen's maid. I'll tell her that my sister is ill and I have to go and see her, and I'll ask if I could leave a kist, a chest full of my valuables, in her bedroom overnight for safekeeping.'

With no trouble at all, the hen-wife got the queen's permission to put the kist in the royal bedroom, and it was installed with the captain hidden inside.

The queen was tired. She was hoping that her husband would return home, but there was no sign of him, so she took the gold ring from her finger and the gold chain from around her neck, and put them on the dressing table; and then she went to bed. When the man in the kist heard her snoring, he slipped out, took the gold ring and the gold chain, and popped back into the kist.

Early next morning the hen-wife came for her kist. It was taken from the queen's room and, as soon as he was able, the captain let himself out and went down to his ship.

'Well,' said the king, who hadn't slept all night, 'what happened?' The captain didn't speak. He just took the ring and the chain out of his pocket and waved them in front of the king. The king found it hard to say anything at all. He thought his wife had been unfaithful, and he had lost his house and lands, so he asked the captain to take him over to the other side of the loch, where he would have to fend for himself in a foreign land. The captain agreed, and ferried the king over the loch. Neither of them spoke a word.

When the captain returned he went straight to the king's house and installed himself there. The king didn't come home and, with a strange man suddenly acting as if he owned the place, the queen didn't know what to do with herself. She dressed up in men's clothing and went down to the shore. There she met a boat and asked to be taken over to the other side. Once across the water she walked until she came to a gentleman's house. She knocked on the door and asked if the master wanted a stable boy. The answer came back that he did, so she was taken in and given a job.

Every night an empty barn on the farm was invaded by a herd of wild beasts, led by a man whose beard was so thick it covered the whole of his face. The stable lad – who, of course, was really the queen in disguise – asked the master if she could go with one of his gillies to catch the wild man. The master said that it was nothing to do with him, and that the wild man wasn't doing any harm, so the stable lad took things into her own hands. She went with some of the gillies and hid in the barn and, when the wild things came in, they captured the man. They took him into the house and shaved off his beard, and there was her husband. She pretended not to know him, and he didn't recognise her because she was disguised as a man.

The next day she went to the master and told him the work was too heavy. She asked if she might get some help, and the master agreed that she could take on the wild man; so the two of them worked together in the stables, without the king realising that he was now his wife's gillie.

Not long after this, the stable lad who was a queen asked the master if she could go and visit friends. The master said she could, and agreed that she should take her gillie with her, together with her wages. On the way, she asked the gillie, her husband, what he was doing with the wild beasts, or what he had done before, but he didn't reply. After a while they came to a familiar inn. He said he couldn't go in, and she asked him why not.

'The innkeeper lent me fifty pounds.'

'Did you pay him back?'

'I didn't, and he told me that, if it wasn't paid within a year and a day, he'd take a strip of skin off my back, from my head to my foot.'

'Quite right too, but I'm going to stay the night here whatever happens, so I want you to put the horses in the stable.'

He kept his head down and did what she asked, but the innkeeper came out and recognised him. 'So it's you! You've come down in the world. I see you're a gillie now. Am I going to get paid?'

'I don't have any money.'

'Then I'll have my strip of skin.'

They took him inside and were about to take the skin off him, but the girl heard the commotion and came into the room.

She asked what was going on, and they told her about the strip of skin. She ordered them to bring up a square of white linen for him to stand on and, if a single drop of blood fell on it, the innkeeper would have a strip taken from his own back. What could they do? They let him go without punishment.

Early next morning she began to lead him across the road to her father's house. If he was reluctant to go to the inn, he was seven times more reluctant to meet her father again. She asked what the problem was this time. Had he caused offence in that place as well?

'I got a wife here a while ago.'

'What happened to her?'

'I don't know.'

'I'm not surprised people take against you if you keep getting into this kind of trouble.'

Her father came out. He didn't recognise his daughter in her disguise, but he did recognise the man who'd bought her.

'So it's you! What happened to your wife?'

'I don't know where she is.'

'What did you do to her?'

'I lost her.'

They decided that the best thing would be to hang him from a high tree. They would make a party of it, and invite their friends to come and celebrate. When the girl saw all the guests riding into town on their fine horses she asked her father what was going on.

'We're going to hang your gillie. He bought a wife from me, and now he's mislaid her. What else do you think I should do with him?'

She went out among the gentlemen who were riding in, and picked the one with the finest horse. 'How much do you want for that horse?' she asked.

'A hundred pounds and he's yours.'

'I'll take him.'

She bought the horse, then she told her gillie to put a shot through its head.

'Did my gillie pay for his wife?' she asked her father.

'Yes, he did.'

'Then you can let him be. If he paid for her, he can do what he likes with her. I bought that horse and now it belongs to me, dead or alive. I told my gillie to put a shot through its head. Who's going to tell me he or I did anything wrong?'

So they let the gillie go free. What else could they do? The girl went into the house, and told one of her sisters to give her a dress.

'What are you going to do with it?'

'Never mind what I'm going to do with it. If I cause any damage, I'll pay for it.'

As soon as she put on the dress her father and sisters recognised her. When they told her husband he wouldn't believe them, until she stood before him. She changed back into man's clothes, and they started along the road to his old house. 'One last thing,' said the girl. 'We'll stay here tonight. I want you to sit at the top of the stairs and write down every word of the conversation I have with the man of the house.'

The captain was happy to accommodate two travellers, a young man and his gillie. After supper, and a few drams, the gillie went to sit in the shadows at the top of the stairs, while the captain and the young man began to chat.

'I thought this was a king's house,' said the young man, who was really the queen. 'How did you come to land here?'

'You're right,' said the captain, whose tongue had been loosened by the drink. 'There was a king here before me, but it's my place now. As you're a stranger I'll tell you how it happened. It's a great tale of how I fooled the king.' And he told the story, every bit of it.

Next morning the captain had to go to court on some business, and he asked if the young man would like to go along. Maybe afterwards they could go for a drink together. She said she would be delighted to go along to the court, as long as her gillie could come too. So off they went, in the captain's coach.

When the court proceedings were over, the girl asked if she might say a word or two. Permission was granted, and she told her gillie to read out the conversation that had taken place between her and the captain the previous evening. At the end of the testimony, they asked what should happen to the captain, if he was there.

'He is here, and he should be hanged.'

So the captain was hanged, and the girl and the young king got back their house. They threw a big party and the last time I passed by, it was still going on.

On the Run

The principle characters in the following three stories are all forced to spend time as fugitives, and to travel long distances in their attempts to escape justice or revenge.

Malcolm MacIlvain is a splendid example of the Champion, a trained fighter who could be hired to settle scores, provide protection and hunt down fugitives. He travels far and wide as a sword for hire. Although his exploits are probably a gathering together of stories told about a number of heroes, J.F. Campbell gives the specific date of 1685 for the episode with the cattle raiders which comes towards the end of Malcolm's story.

A cave on the west side of Iona is known as the Sheep Stealer's Cave. Mairi MacArthur tells how it came by this name.

The story of the elopement of Deirdre and Naoise, and their flight – accompanied by Naoise's brothers – from the wrath of King Conchobar mac Nessa of Ulster, became one of the key narratives in the Celtic Revival of the nineteenth century. It's believed to have originated over a thousand years ago, and its first appearance in manuscript form is in the *Book of Leinster*, whose compilation was begun around 1160. By the late nineteenth century, Deirdre's tale was widely known in Ireland and Scotland, and the notion that the lovers fled to the Scottish Highlands was well established.

The version here is based on one that was taken down on Barra in 1867 by Alexander Carmichael. Carmichael (1832–1912) was born on the island of Lismore and worked as an exciseman, but his adult life was devoted to the collecting of Gaelic lore, which he gathered together in the celebrated *Carmina Gadelica*, first published in 1900.

The story of Deirdre is closely linked both to Loch Ness and, as here, to Loch Etive. Near Cadderlie, on the west shore of the loch, is Eilean Uisneachan, the legendary site of the hunting lodge built by the three brothers. On the opposite side of Loch Etive is Coille Naoise – Naoise's wood – and Ardeny in Glen Lonan is said to have been named after Naoise's brother Ardan.

Here Alexander Carmichael describes Loch Etive, and talks about an acquaintance's experiences of working among the people who lived in the adjacent glens:

> It is the most varied, the most storied, the most stormy, the most beautiful loch in Scotland. Its two divisions differ greatly. Lower Loch Etive is wider and more varied, expanding here and there into broad bays, and projected into here and there by long peninsulas. On each side, between the edge of the water and the base of the mountains, runs a belt of arable land, irregularly broad, studded with trees and fields, houses and churches. In upper Loch Etive the bases of the towering mountains on each side descend immediately down to the water. They continue thus for twelve miles to the head of Loch Etive, and for six miles more to the head of Glen Etive. Loch and glen resemble a huge, deep railway cutting, through which the winds blow up or down during the years and the ages.
>
> Loch Etive … means wild, stormy, raging, and no name could be more appropriate here, for Loch Etive is the dread of men who have to navigate its dark waters in sailing vessels, from the suddenness, fierceness, and contrariness with which the whirling winds come down through the glens and ravines, and from the scarred mountain summits, moving everything that is movable in their path.
>
> The district of Loch Etive is deeply identified with Deirdre and the sons of Uisne. The old people who lived on the sides and at the head of Loch Etive, in the glens which run back, some of them for miles, among the mountains, spoke much of Deirdre. I know of this from Duncan Macniven, who spent his long life as an itinerant

teacher among these almost inaccessible glens, which were tenanted by strong, robust people of clear, retentive memories. Alas, hardly one of these native people is now left on the land – all having been cleared away.

Duncan Macniven said that when he was sent, while still a youth, to teach there, 'the people were big, powerfully built people of bone and muscle. The old people were full of old stories, and of old rhymes, many of them scarcely Christian, but very grand all the same. The stories and poems were about everything – the sun and moon and stars, the beasts and birds and fishes, old feuds and battles and old cattle-raids. I was instructed to unteach these, and to teach the Bible and the Catechism. The people were most kind and most civil to me, and striving who should show me most hospitality. They listened politely to my Bible stories, but when I condemned their Pagan stories and poems about Ossian, and Oscar, and Fionn, and Cumhal, and Cuchulain, and their wild beliefs in the miracles of Calumcille and the other saints, the old people hardly disguised their impatience and resentment. I suppose, like most men who have, or think they have, a mission, I was more earnest than discreet, full of my own beliefs and importance, and intolerant of the beliefs of others. But the old people of those remote glens were grand people, with all their old faults and wild beliefs.'

~ Deirdre and the Sons of Uisne ~

Colum Cruitere – Colum the Harper – was a well-respected and well-to-do musician. He and his wife had no children, and, as they were both getting on, they were sure they never would have any.

Colum heard that a travelling fortune-teller was in the area. When the man called at the house, Colum invited him in, and asked him to tell what the future might hold. The fortune-teller said that he would go outside; and that, when he came back in again, he would have a question for Colum. It wasn't long before the fortune-teller returned, and asked Colum whether he had any children.

'No, there have never been children here, and we don't expect to have any now. There's just my wife and myself. As you can see, we're getting on in years.'

'That's strange,' said the fortune-teller. 'My vision was that you would have a daughter who would cause untold havoc and slaughter throughout Ireland, and that the three greatest heroes in the land would lose their lives because of her.'

'Are you trying to make a fool of me?' said Colum.

'No, that's what I saw.'

'In that case, you can keep your visions to yourself, for I don't think much of them.'

'I saw the whole thing very clearly.'

'It's just not possible,' said Colum. 'My wife and I are too old to have children, and that's all there is to it. I'm sure you're good enough at what you do, but I don't want to hear any more of your ridiculous predictions.'

The fortune-teller went on his way and, not long after, Colum the Harper's wife became pregnant. As she grew heavier, Colum's mood became more and more dark. All day he was restless, and he couldn't sleep at night. He began to feel completely adrift, without friends, guidance or support of any kind, and he regretted terribly that he hadn't paid more attention to the fortune-teller, for he was now convinced that everything the man had told him would come true. Colum began to fret continually as to how he could prevent the bloodshed and mayhem that had been predicted. He decided that, if the child arrived, he would need to keep her hidden in a place where she would never be seen or heard.

Colum's wife did give birth to a baby girl. The only person Colum allowed anywhere near the house was the nurse, the midwife who had been at the birth. Colum asked if she would be willing to bring up the child in secret, in a far-off place, and the woman said she would do whatever she was able to keep the child from the eyes and ears of men.

Colum the Harper went with three men to a distant spot among the mountains, where they hollowed out a grassy mound with their spades, and lined it inside so it was a cosy little place to live in.

Then he sent the nurse and the baby to this wild, remote sheiling where no one would see or hear Deirdre, for that was the name of the child. Colum made sure everything was prepared for them. He sent food and clothing to last a year, and promised the nurse that more provisions would be sent every twelve months for as long as he was alive. And he kept his word.

Deirdre and the nurse lived by themselves in the little sheiling among the mountains, and no one, apart from Colum and his wife, knew that they were there. By the time she was fourteen, Deirdre was as lithe and fair as a young sapling, and straight as a stem of rush growing on the moorland. Her beauty was outstanding, her skin was as white and smooth as swansdown, and she moved with the elegance of a hind on the hill. She was prone to blushing, and the fire would rise into her cheeks for the smallest reason. The nurse taught Deirdre everything she knew about the natural world – the plants that sprang from the earth, the birds that carolled in the bushes, the sparkling stars – but she told her nothing of other human beings.

One wild, wintry night, when the clouds were rampaging across the sky, a hunter came to the green mound. He was exhausted.

He had been hunting all day, and had become separated from his companions, and now he lay down to shelter on the side of the knoll where Deirdre lived. Hunger, tiredness and cold overtook him, and he fell into a deep sleep. He dreamed that the knoll was a *sìthean* – a fairy hill – and that he was inside it, enjoying the warmth, the hospitality, and the music. In his sleep, the hunter called out that, if anyone was in the mound, in the name of the God of the Elements, would they let him in?

Deirdre heard the voice that was coming from outside in the storm. She asked the nurse what it was.

'It's nothing to concern you. The birds have been separated and they're trying to find each other again. Leave them be. Let them fly off and join their companions in the forest.'

The hunter dreamed again, and called out as before, that if there was anyone in the mound, to let him in. Again, Deirdre asked what the voice was, and again the nurse told her it was the birds searching for their friends.

A third time the hunter called out in his sleep that he was frozen and hungry, and, if there was anyone in the knoll, to let him in, in the name of the God of the Elements. Deirdre asked a third time what the voice was, and a third time the nurse replied that it was the birds, and to let them fly on their way, for there was no shelter for them in the sheiling.

'Oh nurse, you've always told me that if anything should be asked in the name of the God of the Elements, it must be done,' Deirdre said. 'Even though you say there's no room in here for that cold, hungry bird, I must do as you've taught me; so I'll let it in myself.'

Deirdre got up and unbarred the door, and let in the hunter. She brought out food and drink, and told him to sit and eat.

'When I came in here,' said the hunter, 'I was desperate for food and drink and warmth. Now I've seen you, my desire for any of these things has completely vanished.'

'You have what you need,' the nurse said. 'Be grateful that you were given hospitality, and when you go, don't you dare tell a soul what you've seen here tonight, or you'll have me to reckon with.'

'Maybe I will keep quiet about what I've seen. But, by the God of the Elements, I must tell you that there are folk who would have this exquisite creature out of here in an instant, if they knew where you were hiding her.'

'Who are these people?' asked Deirdre.

'They are Naoise, son of Uisne, and Aillean and Ardan, his two brothers.'

'What do these brothers look like?'

'They have hair as black as a raven's feathers, skin white as the swan on the water, and cheeks as red as the blood of the fawn. They are as strong as the salmon swimming against the stream, and stately as the stag on the hill. And Naoise stands head and shoulders above anyone else in Ireland.'

'Never mind who they are,' said the nurse. 'I want you out of here and down that road. I'm sorry that you came by, and even more sorry that she let you in.'

The hunter left. As he was travelling along, it occurred to him that Conachar the King of Ulster had no one to share his bed or join him in conversation, and that he might give a good reward to know that such a beauty was living secretly in that remote place. He went straight to Conachar's palace and sent a message to the king that he had news that might be of interest.

The king came out of the palace to speak with the hunter. 'What news is this that you've brought me?'

'Your majesty, I thought you would like to know that I have just seen the most beautiful girl in the whole of Ireland.'

'Who is this girl? Where can I see her? How do you even know she exists – if it's the truth you're telling?'

'It is the truth, your majesty, but I'm the only one who can take you to where she lives.'

'If you can take me there, you'll be well rewarded.'

'I will take you there, though it may cause some upset.'

'Stay in the palace tonight,' said the king. 'First thing tomorrow morning we'll take a party, and you can show me the place.'

Conachar sent secret word to the men of his closest family, including his cousins, the three sons of Fearachar, son of Ro, to let them know what he had planned. The birds carolled in the bushes that bright May morning, but Conachar was awake and up before them, scattering the dew from the grasses as he and his companions headed for the green sheiling among the distant hills. It was a hard way. By the end of the day the men who had been springing along like young bucks at the start of the journey were tired by the track and torn by the briars, staggering along as they clung to each other for support.

They came to the top of a hill and looked down on the sheiling. 'There it is,' said the hunter. 'I'm not going any further. If the old woman sees me, she'll kill me.'

Conachar and his band went down to the sheiling. Conachar knocked on the door. From inside, the nurse called out that she wouldn't answer to anybody, and that they should go away and leave her alone.

'If you open up,' said Conachar, 'I'll make sure you get a better place to live than this hovel.'

'I'm happy where I am. I don't want to live anywhere else, being told when to come and where to go. It would take a king and his army to shift me from this little hut tonight.'

'If you don't open up of your own accord,' said Conachar, 'I'll make you open up.'

'Who is it that's ordering me to do this?'

'I'll enlighten you, woman. It's Conachar the King of Ulster – have no doubts about it.'

When she heard who it was, the nurse opened the door. The king entered, and the rest of the party squeezed in after him.

As soon as the king saw Deirdre he wanted nothing else in the world. He was a prisoner of his heart. He and his men took her on their shoulders, and away they went, back to the palace.

Conachar planned to marry Deirdre immediately, but when the idea was put to her, she didn't even understand what was meant, for he was the first man she'd seen outside the darkness of the inside of the sheiling. She didn't know what it meant to be a wife, or even how a young girl was expected to behave. She didn't know how to sit properly on a chair, or what to do in company, for she had never been among crowds of people before.

In spite of Conachar's eagerness, Deirdre asked him to give her a year and a day to get used to the idea of marriage. Conachar only agreed on condition that she promised to marry him at the end of the year, and Deirdre agreed to this. The king put her in a house, hired a governess to look after her education, and made sure she spent both day and night in the company of well-brought-up young women, who would entertain her and keep her busy with conversation. Deirdre took to her new life and, when he visited, Conachar thought he had never seen anything so pleasing or so enchanting.

Deirdre and her attendants were out one day on the hill behind the house, enjoying the sun, when they saw three men in the distance, coming towards them along the track. Deirdre stared at them, wondering who they were. As they got closer, she remembered the words of the hunter, and she knew that they must be the three sons of Uisne, and that the one who was head and shoulders above the other two was Naoise.

The three brothers passed by without even noticing the girls up on the hill, but Deirdre's love for Naoise was so overwhelming that she could do nothing but go after him. She lifted up her skirts and started to run down the hill, and she didn't care at all what her companions thought.

Aidan and Aillean had heard of this legendary beauty, reared in the wilds, that Conachar had captured. They understood their brother Naoise well, and they knew that, if he ever saw her, he would want her for himself, especially as she wasn't yet married to the king. Naoise hadn't noticed Deirdre running towards them, but his brothers had, and each began to urge the other to walk faster, as they had a long way to go, and night was coming on.

From a distance, Deirdre called, 'Naoise, son of Uisne, will you leave me now?'

'What's that sound?' Naoise asked his brothers. 'It seems like someone is calling my name.'

'It's only the ducks on Conachar's royal lake. We should hurry. There's a long way to go, and night is falling fast.'

The brothers put more ground between themselves and Deirdre, but she called after them a second time. 'Naoise, Naoise, son of Uisne, will you leave me now?'

Again, Naoise asked his brothers what the voice was. 'It goes right to my heart. I would answer, but I don't have the words.'

'It's just the cries of Conachar's geese in flight,' the brothers answered. 'Keep going. The dark is coming fast.'

A third time, Deirdre called. 'Naoise, Naoise, Naoise, son of Uisne, will you leave me now?'

'What is it that's calling out?' said Naoise. 'Of all the sounds I've ever heard, that cry is the sweetest and yet the most full of pain.'

'It's nothing more than the cry of the swans on Conachar's lake.'

'Three cries of distress now. I can't go on until I find out where they came from.'

When Naoise and Deirdre met, Deirdre gave three kisses to Naoise and one to each of his brothers, and the blood flowed up into her cheeks as swiftly as the leaves of the aspen shake with the wind. As soon as Naoise saw Deirdre he wanted nothing else in the world. He was a prisoner of his heart, and he gave himself to her utterly. He lifted Deirdre on to his shoulders, and told his brothers to walk on.

Naoise knew that Conachar would be livid at what had happened, even though no marriage had taken place, and that, as they were closely related, the king would take it doubly hard. So Deirdre and the sons of Uisne crossed the sea to Scotland, and found a safe place in the heights of Glen Etive, in a tower where they could catch salmon from the door and shoot deer out of the window.

At the end of the twelve months, when the marriage was due to take place, Conachar was thinking that he would go and take Deirdre by force, whether she was married to Naoise or not. He came up with a plan to invite all his relatives to a great banquet. There he would challenge Naoise to fight, and wrest Deirdre from him. But Conachar thought that it would take more than a simple invitation to lure Naoise back to Ireland, so he decided to send his uncle, Fearachar, son of Ro, to ask on his behalf, and to say that Conachar would have no peace if the sons of Uisne were not at the feast.

Fearachar crossed the sea with his three sons, and made his way to the tower in Glen Etive. The sons of Uisne made them welcome, and asked what news there was of home. 'Good news,' said Fearachar. 'Conachar is planning a feast to entertain his family and friends from the furthest corners of Ireland, and he asked me to tell you that, if the Children of Uisne – his own brothers' sons – don't sit down with him at the table, by the sky above, and the earth below, and by the sun that sets in the west, he will have no peace.'

'We'll go with you,' said Naoise, and his brothers agreed.

'My three sons will accompany you, to make sure you stay safe,' said Fearachar, and the three sons agreed.

'Better freedom in Scotland,' said Deirdre, 'than house arrest in Ireland.'

Fearachar came back. 'Better to be in the home country than to live in exile. It's an unhappy man who gets up in the morning and looks out on a strange land, and who sleeps at night among foreigners.'

'Home means more to me than kin,' said Naoise, 'but we have a good life here.'

'You'll be safe with us,' said Fearachar.

'We'll go with you,' said Naoise.

Deirdre begged Naoise not to return to Ireland. She had a vision and made a song:

I hear the sound of howling dogs
Among the shadows of the night
Fearachar comes with false promises
Conachar glowers from the top of his tower
Conachar glowers from the top of his tower

Naoise fights without an army
Aillean without his clanging shield
No targe or glistening sword for Ardan
Darkness falls on the sons of Uisne
Darkness falls on the sons of Uisne

Put no trust in the words of Fearachar
Conachar's lips are fringed with blood
The brothers lie with their backs to the earth
Deirdre's tears upon their corpses
Deirdre's tears upon their corpses

'I never, myself, paid much attention to the howling of dogs or women's fantasies,' Fearachar said to Naoise. 'Conachar has sent you a special invitation to the feast, and he would be worse than offended if you refused to accept.'

'You're right. We'll go with you.'

Deirdre looked into Naoise's eyes. 'I had another vision. Tell me what it means.' They passed the song between them:

I saw three white doves, with three drops of honey in their mouths
Naoise, son of Uisne, shine light on this dark vision.

It's only a nightmare, Deirdre
The flower of a woman's melancholy.

I saw three savage hawks, drinking the blood of heroes
Naoise, son of Uisne, shine light on this dark vision.

It's only a nightmare, Deirdre
The flower of a woman's melancholy.

I saw three ravens with the leaves of the yew in their beaks
Naoise, son of Uisne, shine light on this dark vision.

It's only a nightmare, Deirdre
The flower of a woman's melancholy.

Naoise said, 'Deirdre, Conachar has invited us to the feast, and it would be uncivil if we didn't attend.'

'If there's any trouble,' said Fearachar, 'my sons and I will be right behind you.' And his sons agreed. Fearachar said that, if any harm should come to the Children of Uisne, he and his boys would sever the head from the body of every Irish warrior.

Deirdre didn't want to leave Glen Etive, but she went with Naoise. She sang a sad song of farewell to the lochs and glens, as they sailed for Ireland.

As soon as the Children of Uisne landed in Ireland, Fearachar sent word to Conachar that they had arrived, and to make sure that he treated them fairly.

'To be honest,' said Conachar, 'I didn't think they would come, even though they were invited. I'm not quite ready for them. There's a place where the mercenaries lodge. They can stay there for the night, and we'll be ready to receive them tomorrow.'

Fearachar passed on the king's message. 'If that's where Conachar wants us to go,' said Naoise, 'we have no choice. But I doubt he's putting us among mercenaries because of his great love for us.'

They got to the house, and it was crammed full of tough soldiers. When Deirdre and the sons of Uisne, together with the sons of Fearachar, entered the place, every man in there laughed. Naoise replied by laughing twice as loud as any of them. One by one the mercenaries stood up, and each of them put a bar on the door. Naoise replied by putting two bars on the door.

The leader of the mercenaries wondered aloud, 'Who is this brave soul who laughs louder than any of us, and puts two bars on the door?'

'I'll answer you,' said Naoise, 'if you tell me what it was that made you laugh when we came in, and why did you bar the door?'

'I'll tell you, hero. I've never seen anyone quite like you come in to this place, and I've never seen men I would so much like to chew up and spit out, as I would like to chew up and spit out the six of you. But just explain to me – when we laughed at you, why did you laugh even louder, and when each of us barred the door once, why did you bar it twice?'

'To be truthful, I've never seen any company, living or dead, whose heads I would more like to separate from their bodies.'

Naoise stood, head and shoulders above the rest of them. He began to scythe through the mercenaries like a slaughtering machine, and in a short time not a single one of them was left alive. Then he and his brothers, Deirdre, and the sons of Fearachar tidied up the bodies, cleaned the house, built a fire, and made themselves comfortable for the night.

The next morning, Conachar was wondering why he'd had no word from the mercenaries. He told the nurse to go down and find out what was happening. 'See if Deirdre still looks as young and beautiful as she did when she left me. If she is, I'll use lance and sword to get her back, whatever those brothers throw at me. If she's lost her bloom, Naoise can keep her.'

The nurse went down to the mercenaries' quarters. She managed to peep inside through a small chicken hole in the door, and returned to Conachar to report what she had seen. 'The marks of hardship and sorrow are so plain on her, she scarcely looks like the same person. There's very little left of Deirdre's bloom and beauty.'

Conachar wasn't convinced. He sent another spy, the King of Lochlann's son, who was there for the feast. The lad went down to the mercenaries' quarters, and peeped in through the chicken hole.

Deirdre and the others were playing a game of dice when Deirdre saw an eye staring at her through the hole, and the fire rose up through her cheeks. Naoise noticed her blushes. He turned and saw the eye. He picked up one of the dice, sent it flying through the hole in the door, and blinded the King of Lochlann's son.

The lad returned to the palace, and Conachar asked him what was wrong. 'You were happy enough when you went down there. Have you seen Deirdre? How does she look?'

'I've seen her alright, and while I was looking at her through the chicken hole, Naoise the son of Uisne put out my eye with a dice. But if I hadn't promised to come back here, I would happily have stayed to gaze on her with my other eye.'

'That's what I thought,' said Conachar. He sent three hundred great warriors down to the mercenaries' quarters, with orders to kill the sons of Uisne and the sons of Fearachar and to bring Deirdre back.

'They're coming for us,' said Deirdre. 'I can hear them.'

'I'll go out and meet them,' said Naoise.

'No,' said Boinne the Fierce, the first son of Fearachar, 'I'll go. I promised my father before he went home that I wouldn't let any harm come to you.'

Boinne the Fierce went out and slaughtered a hundred warriors. From high on the hill the king shouted, 'Who is it down there killing all my men?'

'I'm Boinne the Fierce, first son of Fearachar.'

'I gave land to your grandfather, I gave land to your father, and I'll give you land if you'll come over to me.'

'I accept your offer,' said Boinne, and joined the king's men.

'He's gone over to Conachar,' said Deirdre.

'He may have gone over, but he did good work before he went,' said Naoise.

Conachar sent down three hundred more warriors. Naoise said he would go out to meet them, but Fearachar's second son, Cuilionn, the Iron Man, went in his place. After Cuilionn had slaughtered two thirds of the warriors, Conachar offered him the same deal he'd offered to Boinne, and Cuilionn accepted.

Three hundred more warriors were sent to kill the brothers and bring back Deirdre. This time Fearachar's third son, Fillan the Faithful, went out to meet them. He cut a magnificent figure in his battle-gear, polished and gleaming, glittering with images of birds, beasts and creeping things – the eagle, the lion and the serpent. And Fillan destroyed the whole of Conachar's army.

Conachar rushed out of his palace, furious, and shouted down to ask who was responsible for the slaughter. 'Fillan the Faithful, third son of Fearachar,' was the reply. Conachar offered a gift of land, as he'd offered land to Fillan's two brothers before him.

'I won't accept your land. I'd rather go home and be able to tell my father I kept my promise to him, than take anything you could possibly offer me. The sons of Uisne are as close kin to me as they are to you, Conachar, and I believe, if you could have your way, you'd see us all dead.

Fillan went back to the house, and said that he would return home to tell his father that the sons of Uisne were now safe from the hands of the king. It was almost dawn, and Naoise decided they should leave the house and return to Scotland.

When daylight came, word reached Conachar that Deirdre and the sons of Uisne were no longer in the house of the mercenaries. He sent out men to hunt them down, and then he called for Duanan Gacha, his personal magician. 'I paid a lot for your education and training,' he said. 'I hope it was a wise investment. Turn your attention to the ones who disrespected me, who crept away in the night, who I have no power to turn back.'

'I can slow them down until your hunters catch up with them,' said the magician. He cast up a forest in the path of the fugitives, but Naoise took Deirdre by the hand, and they came through easily.

'Not good enough,' said Conachar. 'They don't slow down, and they don't get knocked off course. They just keep going.'

'I'll try something else,' said the magician, and as Deirdre and the brothers ran across the green plain, he filled it with a grey sea. The sons of Uisne took off their clothes and tied them in bundles behind their heads, Naoise took Deirdre on his back, and they plunged into the sea and began to swim.

'Better,' said Conachar. 'But they still keep going, defying me, thinking only of themselves.'

'I'll try again,' said the magician. He put a spell on the grey sea, and the water froze into jagged lumps, sharp as swords and poisonous as serpents.

Ardan was the first to begin to tire. Naoise took his brother on to his right shoulder, but it was only a short while before he died. Even though Ardan was dead, Naoise wouldn't let go of him. Aillean called out that he couldn't keep going much longer. Naoise told him to cling on and he would get him to the land, but it wasn't long before Aillean's grip loosened. When Naoise saw that his two brothers were gone he gave up the struggle, lay down and took his last breath.

'I've done as you asked,' said the king's magician. 'The Children of Uisne are dead. They won't bother you any more; and your sweetheart, your bride-to-be, is alive and well.'

'Great credit to you, and great benefit to me. The fortune I spent on your education and training was more than justified,' said the king. 'Now dry out the sea, so I can look at Deirdre.' The sea drained away and there were the sons of Uisne, lying side by side on the green machair, and Deirdre weeping over the corpses.

The king told the people who had gathered there to dig a pit and lay the brothers in it, side by side. Deirdre sat next to the grave asking again and again for it to be dug long and wide. When the work was over, and the bodies had been lowered in, she called on the sons of Uisne, if the dead could hear, to move over and make room for her. There was a shifting of shadows deep in the pit, and then Deirdre threw herself down into the darkness. She lay there, dead at Naoise's side.

Conachar ordered Deirdre's body to be taken out of the grave and buried on the far side of Loch Etive. After a while, a young pine grew out of Deirdre's grave, and another sprang out of the burial mound of the sons of Uisne. As the trees became taller, they leant towards each other, until they intertwined above the middle of the loch. Twice, Conachar ordered them to be cut down, but when he married, his wife told him to put an end to this meddling in the affairs of the dead, and so he left the past behind forever.

~ The Sheep Stealer's Cave ~

Its Gaelic name is Uamh a' Bhodaich – the Old Fellow's Cave – and no one chances on it easily. In fact, you would need a climber's skill and nerve to clamber up the cliffs beyond Spouting Cave, on Iona's south-west coast, to a grassy ledge looking directly out to the broad Atlantic. Behind you, now much eroded, is the cave once described to Lord Archibald Campbell as 'about the size of an ordinary Highland dwelling house'. A split in the roof served as a chimney in this craggy cottage with its grand sea view. It was local guide John MacDonald who, in 1885, told Campbell how the cave got its name.

An old fellow had taken refuge in it, no one knew for how long. The entrance was not visible from any house and he must have taken care to dampen smoke seeping up through the rock vent from an occasional driftwood fire. But a local woman, searching for a lost sheep, made for this very coast, aware that an animal might get trapped in its gullies or fall from its precipices. She came on the chimney and looked down. A man she had never seen before looked up – he was in the act of killing a sheep, her missing sheep.

'*Thig an nuas*,' he said coolly, 'Come on down.'

'I will,' she replied, just as nonchalantly, but then took to her heels as fast as she could over the rocks and rough grassland. In those days everyone lived in the old village, clustered on the island's east side, so it was over a mile to her own home and safety. At one point she felt her pursuer tug at the edge of her shawl, and she let it drop to the ground. At a hillock close by a field where her brothers were working, she collapsed, blurted out the story and died of exhaustion.

The stranger had already fled to the shore, where it turned out he had hidden a boat, and got clean away. Later, the locals heard that he was from Islay and was in hiding after committing a murder there. No one ever knew whose coast he landed on next. The rocky hideout is also known as the Sheep Stealer's Cave and the little hill where the woman died is called Cnoc na h-Analach, literally the Hill of the Breath.

Big Malcolm MacIlvain

There was a time when the MacNeills were in possession of the land around Loch Eck, in Cowal. The story goes that one MacNeill kept his sons close to him, and when they married he gave them land. The sons did the same for their sons, and soon all the folk who lived in Stratheck were related to each other. They didn't have a lot to do with outsiders, as they were sure that they themselves were the best and kindest people around. However, there's an old saying that, 'There is no forest without withered branches,' and it's true that when the best of friends fall out, it can be the worst of situations.

One day the MacNeills decided they would go fishing together on the river Eachaig. There were hordes of them. A forester, a MacIlvain, was standing on the mountain slopes looking down, when a woman he'd not seen before passed by. 'There's a great number of the MacNeills fishing on the river today,' he said to the woman. 'I've counted nearly a hundred of them, and there are still more.'

'There may be many of them fishing today,' the woman replied, 'but there won't be so many tomorrow. This is the last time you'll see so many MacNeills fishing on the banks of the Eachaig.'

The woman went away, and the forester didn't know who she was, where she came from, or where she'd gone; but when he looked back at the river, the members of the Clan Neill were fighting amongst themselves. The wife of the eldest brother had taken against the youngest brother, and told her husband that the boy had tried to molest her. The older brother met the youngest at the river and, without giving him any reason, drew his sword and challenged him. Members of the family who were nearby ran to try and calm the situation, but the oldest killed the youngest, then he himself was wounded by the folk who'd tried to separate them.

All of the MacNeills dropped their rods and drew their swords, scarcely bothering to find out who it was they were fighting, or wondering which side they were on, and many of them were killed. After the fighting had ended, people stood around asking how this could have happened. Only two or three of them were able to say how it began, with the poisonous words of the elder brother's wife. They were all truly sorry, but it was too late to bring back the dead.

That was the end of the MacNeills in that part of Argyll. The few surviving men left Stratheck and went their separate ways, and they never spoke to each other again. It became proverbial that, if people were great friends and then fell out with each other, they were like the MacNeills.

Some of the women married the men of the Clan Ilvain, who took over the land after the MacNeills left.

The MacIlvains thrived in Stratheck, and gained a great reputation as brave and respected men. One in particular, Big Malcolm MacIlvain, became famous for his strength and his exploits, and for his skill as a swordsman. He lived on the shores of Loch Eck, but stravaiged far and wide, and when he was travelling by Loch Goil he fell in love with a girl who lived in those parts. Whenever he went to visit her he couldn't be bothered to walk all the way around Loch Eck so, being a good swimmer, he would take off his clothes, tie them behind his head, and swim across the water.

There was said to be a Water Bull in the loch. Folk were terrified of this creature, which they claimed was uncharacteristically quite as sinister as a Water Horse. It came out of the loch at night and ate the corn in the surrounding fields. It was also reputed to eat people; but Big Malcolm wasn't in the least afraid. He kept his sword on when he crossed Loch Eck, not scared of the Water Bull or of any other danger; and, when he crossed over the moor at night to meet his girlfriend, he wasn't bothered by the possibility of meeting witches or similar supernatural beings.

One night, when Malcolm was swimming across the loch, he saw a huge black shape coming towards him. He thought it was the Water Bull but, when it got closer, he realised it was a real bull, made of flesh and blood. Malcolm drew his sword, thinking to make the bull turn back, but the creature kept coming, so there was a fight in the middle of the loch. The fight ended when the bull, having had its ears sliced off, retreated the way it had come. Malcolm carried on and, when he reached the far shore, he started over the moor to join his sweetheart. He was exhausted from the battle with the bull so, when he came to a ditch, he thought he would lie down in it and take a rest. He was so tired he fell asleep and, in the morning, his sweetheart found him, curled up and snoring. She went to the house and brought everyone back to make fun of him. When he woke, they were all pointing at him, laughing and mocking.

That was the last time Malcolm ever went to see the woman who lived by Loch Goil. Word got round about what had happened, and her reputation never recovered. No man ever visited her again, and she died alone.

When Malcolm got back home, he told his neighbours that the bull which had been eating their corn was real enough, and had been swimming over from the other side of the loch. If they didn't believe him they should be able to identify it, since both its ears were missing. Sure enough the bull was found, though it was so terrified by the battle with Big Malcolm that it never crossed the loch again. And so the proverb sprang up, referring to the very end of something, that 'Big Malcolm did not go again, and the bull did not come again'.

In Stratheck there was a man of the Clan Aulay, who had a grown-up son by his first wife. When that wife died the man married again, and his second wife took against the son. She told her husband that the young man had made advances to her. MacAulay was out of his mind with anger. He took his bow and arrows and lay hidden at the side of the road he knew his son would be taking, and, when he passed close by, MacAulay loosed a fatal arrow. The dying boy asked MacAulay why he had shot him, and MacAulay told him what his wife had said about the advances. With his last breath the boy denied the story, and MacAulay realised what a dreadful mistake he had made, a mistake which saddened him until his final days.

After he had killed his son, MacAulay was forced to go on the run. He went into hiding and no one could find out what had happened to him, though many tried. He was a strong man, and good with the sword as well as with the bow. Big Malcolm MacIlvain was considered the best match for him in those parts, so he was given a warrant, with the offer of a reward, to hunt MacAulay down. In fact Malcolm wasn't so keen to catch MacAulay, for he thought that to be forced to become a fugitive, and to have to bear such a burden of grief, was punishment enough for the man. But MacAulay didn't know this; he got the notion that, if Big Malcolm were dead, there would be no one else to fear, for none would dare stand up to him. So he waited for an opportunity to take Malcolm out with an arrow.

One night Malcolm was coming home with a goat over his shoulders. MacAulay was in hiding waiting for him. He shot at Malcolm and the arrow pierced the goat and killed it. Malcolm shouted out, 'You shoot from over there, and cause mayhem over here. If I go over from here, I'll cause mayhem over there.' As Malcolm made no attempt to retaliate, MacAulay took this as meaning that the big man wasn't so interested in capturing him, and he felt ashamed that he had been the first to attack. But he thought that he would be safer far away from Malcolm rather than close by, so he went off to the other side of Loch Fyne, where he became a notorious robber.

The Earl of Argyll sent a messenger to Big Malcolm MacIlvain, telling him that there was a robber called Niall na Gainne – Niall of the Arrow – who was making a nuisance of himself, particularly in Kintyre. Nobody had been able to catch this Niall, and if Malcolm could bring him back he would get any reward he asked for. Malcolm made the journey to the earl's castle in Inveraray, and introduced himself. The earl repeated his offer, that if Malcolm brought back Niall na Gainne he would get the first thing he asked for in return.

So Malcolm set off. He spent the first night in Kilmartin, at an inn that was kept by a man called Taylor. There happened to be another traveller lodging there who was well muscled, large and alert, plainly a champion like Malcolm. Big Malcolm MacIlvain eyed the man, and the man eyed Big Malcolm. Each was keen to know who the other was, but no one in the inn was letting on. The two champions began to drink together, and then they started to quarrel. They wrestled until Malcolm threw the man, and had him pinned to the floor. The man on the floor said, 'I don't know who would be capable of this, apart from Big Malcolm MacIlvain.'

'It is indeed Big Malcolm who's on top of you,' was the reply.

'Your reputation couldn't be higher,' said the man. 'I'm not ashamed to be bested by you. Let me up and I'll do anything you ask.'

Malcolm was convinced that the man was Niall na Gainne, but when they got back to Inveraray it turned out he was another champion called Strong Lachlan. However, since Strong Lachlan was also wanted for robbery, he was thrown in gaol in any case.

Malcolm set off again, with his dog and a gillie, on the trail of Niall na Gainne. They got as far as Lochgilphead, and were told that Niall had gone to a fair in the south of Kintyre. They made for the fair and, as they got closer, people confirmed that Niall had headed that way; but when Malcolm and his gillie got there they couldn't see him. For a while they walked up and down, trying to catch sight of Niall, asking folk if they'd seen him. They had no luck so they decided to go and get a drink. They tied up the dog and went into the tent, got their drinks and sat down, when there was a terrible squealing from outside. The squealing came from Malcolm's dog, which had almost been cut in two. Malcolm was nearly insane with rage. 'Whoever cut the dog with their sword would cut me too!'

A man came up to them. 'It was Niall na Gainne, the man you've been looking for. He was watching you. He waited until you and your companion went into the drinking tent, then he cut the dog and ran away.'

Malcolm asked around and was told that Niall had headed north. 'You go north by the west road,' he told the gillie, 'and I'll go by the east road, and we'll meet at Tarbert House. If you get any news of Niall na Gainne, you can give it to me when we meet.'

When they met in Tarbert neither of them had anything to report. They struck out west, and then heard that Niall and his gillie were camped on the slopes at Sliabh Gaoil in Knapdale. Big Malcolm and his man went there as fast as they could, and found the two renegades preparing a meal. They had killed a young ram, taken out its stomach, filled it with water, and suspended it over a fire, and they were boiling some of the ram's flesh in the water. Malcolm and his gillie crept up on them, and as soon as Niall saw them he realised that it was his long-awaited nemesis. At the same time, Malcolm realised that Niall na Gainne was none other than the fugitive MacAulay. Hunter and hunted drew their swords and began to fight. The gillies drew their swords too, but neither did anything except gape at their masters and at each other.

After a while Malcolm and MacAulay stopped fighting and faced each other, holding their ground like two great bulls in combat. Then Malcolm rushed forward, and grabbed MacAulay's sword by the hilt. They began to wrestle, and MacAulay was felled. The two gillies started to fight, but Malcolm's man was able to subdue MacAulay's. When MacAulay saw this, he surrendered. Malcolm tied him up, and they started off on the long walk to justice.

When they got close to Inveraray, MacAulay told Malcolm that, if he would let him go free, MacAulay would give him a better reward than he could get off the earl. Malcolm asked him what he meant, and MacAulay replied that he had stolen the land charters from many of the lairds in Kintyre, and that he would hand them over in return for his freedom.

'Where are the charters?' asked Malcolm.

'I have them with me,' MacAulay replied. Malcolm told him that the charters should go back to their owners, and that, if MacAulay would promise on his honour to give up robbery, he would try and find a way to get him set free. MacAulay agreed, saying that he had only become a brigand as a result of hard circumstance; if he could be pardoned he would be more than willing to go back to his old life, for he had never been happier than when he was farming.

When they reached Inveraray, the charters were handed over to the Earl of Argyll, who put them to one side. The earl then repeated his promise that he would give Big Malcolm whatever he asked for, so long as it wasn't the earl's estate. Argyll would rather have hanged MacAulay, but he was as good as his word. He agreed to Malcolm's request to let Niall go free, with Malcolm's surety that MacAulay would never rob again. So Malcolm delivered MacAulay back home to his family, even though he was the man who had previously shot dead a goat on Malcolm's shoulders.

Strong Lachlan spent some time in prison, but he was released after he promised to mend his ways.

About the charters, nothing more was said. The Earl of Argyll kept them, and, after his death, his successor found them and didn't know how they had come to be there. He claimed the lands as his own, and dispossessed the people who were living on them.

On a farm called Ard na Blath – the Flower Height – at the east side of Loch Eck, lived a well-respected man who had married a much younger woman. Big Malcolm got the notion that he wanted the woman for himself, even though she was already married, so he kidnapped her and hid her in a cave near Bernice, on the other side of the loch. When he was away, Malcolm would place a huge stone flag over the mouth of the cave to stop the woman escaping, and neither her husband nor anyone else knew what had become of her.

One day Malcolm set off on a journey and, as usual, he put the stone flag over the mouth of the cave. After he left, a traveller passed by. The woman heard the tramp of feet, and called out, and the traveller heard her voice. He went to the cave and called to ask who she was; she told him her name, and that she was being kept prisoner by Big Malcolm MacIlvain. The man tried to shift the flag, but it wouldn't budge, so he went as fast as he could to the Flower Height, to tell the woman's husband. The husband returned to the cave with a band of men. They took away the stone flag and released the woman, but seven of them didn't have the strength to put the flag back in place.

The man from the Flower Height took his wife home, and started proceedings against Big Malcolm. Other folk with grievances came forward, and armed men were sent to capture him, so he fled to the Lowlands, and landed at a farm in New Kilpatrick in Dunbartonshire. The men were all away, and the woman of the house told Malcolm she could give him a billet in the barn, and a blanket to keep him warm. She sent a boy along with a candle to light the way. From the boy's accent, Big Malcolm could tell that he was a Highlander, and he asked him in Gaelic where he was from. The boy told him, and Malcolm replied that he knew the boy's people. Then he made himself a bed among the straw.

The boy went back into the house and told everyone there that the man in the barn was Big Malcolm MacIlvain. When the men returned home, the women passed on the tale. The men were aware that Big Malcolm was a fugitive with a price on his head, and one of the servants knew that his pursuers were not far away. The servant went and betrayed Malcolm, who hadn't been long asleep when the little boy came to the barn with the candle, to show where he lay.

Malcolm woke as soon as his pursuers came in. He drew his sword and struck the candle out of the boy's hand, saying that he would have killed the lad if he hadn't known his people. Malcolm fought his way out of the barn and into the night. If he'd been more familiar with the place he would have escaped, but he soon found himself up to his knees in a bog. He turned and battled with his pursuers until his sword broke, and then he was forced slowly backwards, still defending himself with what was left of the sword, until he was up to his waist in the peaty water. Big Malcolm held out the broken piece of sword to the commander of the pursuers,

offering to surrender but, when the commander went to take the weapon, Malcolm struck him with it on the forehead and killed him. The men went after Malcolm, firing arrows, and the big man was wounded. He realised the game was up, so he threw his bit of sword away and told them they could do as they pleased with him. His hands were tied, and he was taken to Dumbarton and thrown in gaol.

To make sure that he didn't escape, Malcolm was bound in iron chains that weighed seven stones and more. While he was waiting to be tried his friends and relatives visited from time to time, to bring him things that he might need. One of the visitors was a smith who lived at the head of Loch Eck, and was married to Malcolm's sister. The smith had a sharp eye, and observed closely everything that went on in the prison. He noticed that, when the gaoler took a visitor to one of the cells, he would lock them in and leave the key in the lock, then go away until visiting time was over. The smith returned home and told what he had seen. Whenever someone went to visit Big Malcolm in Dumbarton they would check on the gaoler's behaviour, and they all confirmed this habit of leaving the key in the cell door.

One day the smith said to his wife, 'When you go to see your brother, take some stiff barley dough with you, and see if you can get an impression of that key. With a bit of luck I should be able to use it to make a duplicate. Then we can look at springing Big Malcolm from gaol.'

Malcolm's sister did as her husband suggested. It took her a day to get to Dumbarton, and the following day, at noon, she was let into the prison, along with the other visitors. When everyone was inside, the gaoler shut and locked the big door and kept the key in his hand. As usual, when he let people in to the individual cells, he locked them in and left the key in the lock. It happened that Malcolm's was the final cell so, as soon as the door was opened, his sister gave the gaoler some money to bring Big Malcolm a dram and buy one for himself.

The gaoler shut the door of the cell, but left the key in the lock. As soon as he was off on his errand, Malcolm's sister took the key and pressed it into the barley dough. She managed to get it back in the lock, just as she heard the gaoler's footsteps coming towards the cell. When she got home, her husband was able to make a perfect copy of the key from the dough mould.

A few days later Malcolm's sister returned to Dumbarton. She gave her brother a barley bannock with the duplicate key inside, and told him that her husband the smith would be waiting for him with a boat and crew, at the head of the sand on the Cardross side of Leven Water, which was to the west of Dumbarton.

The gaol was in the heart of the town, and its entrance was up a flight of steps. In the middle of the night, when the citizens of Dumbarton were asleep in their beds, Malcolm let himself out of his cell with the forged key and went along the corridor until he found a window. He managed to remove enough of the window to make a hole big enough to squeeze through, and lowered himself down on to the top of the steps using a rope he'd made from his bed sheets. Still bound in chains, he made his way to the boat where the smith was waiting. They rowed to head of Holy Loch, and then Malcolm walked all the way to the forge at the head of Loch Eck, where the smith took a hammer and chisel and released him from his iron fetters. Malcolm realised it would be unsafe to remain there. He took a gillie and went to hide out in a place called the Raven's Rock, in the wilds of Cowal.

Big Malcolm and the gillie had been at Raven's Rock for a good while, when one day the gillie returned with the news that the Laird of Skipness, which is not far from Tarbert, had been challenged by an Irish champion and had accepted the challenge. The day of the fight was already agreed upon. This had come about because, some time before, the Laird of Skipness had been staying in Ireland with a gentleman who had a very beautiful daughter. The gentleman had already decided whom his daughter would be marrying, but she and Skipness had fallen in love, and, when Skipness returned home, the girl went with him. After they were married, Skipness sent word to the Irish gentleman, who was not best pleased that his daughter had got wed without his consent, and that her approved suitor had been slighted. The furious Irishman hired the champion, who was a crack swordsman. They crossed the Irish Sea and sought out Skipness, whom they insulted, together with the Scots in general. Then they challenged him to a sword fight, to which the laird had agreed.

On the allotted day Malcolm and his gillie sailed over Loch Fyne, and they were at Skipness in good time for the start of the fight. The laird was a good swordsman, but no match for the champion, who had never been bested. After a while the laird became short of breath, and asked if there was any among the onlookers who could take over while he got back his wind. There was no response, but many people had recognised Big Malcolm, and they were sidling up to him, telling him to give the laird some respite.

Again the laird called out for assistance, and again no one stepped up. 'See,' said the Irish champion to Skipness, 'now you know who your true friends are.' It was then that Malcolm came forward, drew his sword, and took up the challenge.

The two champions faced each other, and the fight began. At first Big Malcolm stood his ground, but after a while the Irishman began to drive him back into the loch, until he was up to his waist in the water. The Irishman told Malcolm he had to choose between death by the sword or death by drowning. 'I'll take neither,' replied Malcolm. 'I've just been toying with you up till now.' He began to fight his way back out of the loch. It wasn't long before he gave the Irish champion a deadly wound, and finished the matter for good by cutting off his head. The Irish party had nothing to say. They put their champion's body on board one of the boats, and set off back for home.

After his victory, everyone gathered round Big Malcolm, wanting to congratulate him and asking where he'd been. Without thinking he told them he'd been hiding out at Raven's Rock, but he soon realised that this was a mistake, as he was still a wanted man. He decided he would be safer in Ireland, where no one knew him, so he and the gillie took their boat and landed on the island of Rathlin, close to the Antrim coast.

The people of Rathlin Island gave Malcolm and his gillie such a welcome that they thought they might settle there, but one day a traveller passed through who recognised Malcolm as the slayer of the Irish champion. When they heard this, the Rathlin folk took against Malcolm, and plotted to murder him. Big Malcolm always kept his sword by him, and on this occasion he certainly needed it. He and his gillie were too skilled with their weapons for the mob to dare come close, but instead people started to throw stones at them. The stones on Rathlin are flint, and sharp as a razor if they are split. Malcolm tried to make a break through the crowd to get to the beach, and one of them threw a stone which hit him in the mouth and knocked out one of his teeth. Malcolm ran up to the man who was responsible and cut a chunk out of his back. He made up a song:

In the fight I lost a tooth
But I took a strip of his coat away

After this, the Rathlin folk didn't dare attack. Malcolm and his gillie got down to the beach and set sail, and they decided to go back home. If Rathlin was inhospitable, the Irish mainland could only be worse. Eventually they returned to Raven's Rock where they learned of the death of the man Malcolm had torn the strip off.

At this time the men of Atholl and the MacDonalds had been given permission by the king to plunder the lands of the Campbells, and a band of MacDonalds of Keppoch had gone to the south part of Cowal to lift cattle. Big Malcolm MacIlvain heard of this, and that they had also carried off all the cattle from Stratheck. Malcolm set out to see how much his friends there had suffered at the hands of the raiders, and on his journey he met a poor widow whose only cow had been taken. He promised to get the beast back for her, and carried on until he came to a farm in Strachur where the raiders were camped for the night. They had already killed the widow's cow, and were boiling its flesh over a fire using its own stomach as a vessel.

Some of the raiders were close by, vying with each other as to how far they could throw a big stone. Malcolm had been a fugitive for a good while, and he was ragged and dirty with a great growth of beard. He stood looking at the men, who thought he was a beggar wandered in from the night. 'Come on old man,' said one of them. 'See how far you can pitch this thing. I'm sure you'll do well.'

'There was a time when I could have taken you all on,' said Malcolm, 'but I'm not sure I can do much now.' He picked up the stone and threw it as far as any of the MacDonalds had managed.

The captain of the raiders came up. 'Try again, old man. I'll bet you can throw it further than that.' Big Malcolm picked up the stone and threw it even further. 'Go on lads,' said the captain, 'it's your turn now. And don't let him beat you this time.' Then he left them, to take a turn around the cattle.

One of the boys challenged Malcolm to a wrestling match, but Malcolm turned him down. He waited until he thought the captain was far enough away from the rest of them, and then pretended that he was going off again on his travels. But instead he caught up with the captain, grabbed hold of him and felled him. Malcolm sat on top of the captain, brought out his dirk and held it to the man's chest. 'If you move an inch I'll put this through you,' he said.

The raiders heard the scuffling, and ran to see what was going on. When they saw Malcolm on top of their leader, they ran to help, but Malcolm shouted to them that if they came any closer it would be curtains for the captain. On the other hand, if they kept their distance, he and the captain could discuss the situation amicably.

The raiders stayed put, and the captain asked Big Malcolm what it was that he wanted. 'I want you to hand over all the cattle that you've stolen. If you don't, I'll put this dirk through you.'

'Might I ask who it is that dares to speak so boldly to me in front of my men?'

'The name's Big Malcolm MacIlvain. You may have heard of him.'

'Indeed I have heard of him,' said the captain. 'Let me up and you can have all the cattle, except those that have already been killed.'

As soon as the captain was up, his men were at him hoping to persuade him to hang on to the cattle; but he stuck to his word. The captain explained to them who Malcolm was – that he was a great champion, and that it was no disgrace to return the cattle to a man such as him. 'I'm glad to have met you,' he said to Malcolm. 'If you're ever out Keppoch way, call and see me, and you'll get a night's hospitality.'

Malcolm drove the cattle back to Stratheck and returned them to their rightful owners, and he managed somehow to find another cow for the widow. Though Malcolm was forgiven his transgressions after this good deed, he didn't stay by Loch Eck. He went back to Cowal where he got married and became a farmer, and his descendants are living there still.

Bannocks and Banquets

Food and drink play an important part in many of the Argyll stories. For a Highland chieftain, dispensing hospitality was a matter of honour. A praise song, written around 1600 for a MacGregor of Glen Lyon, speaks of:

> Beer in tassies,
> being drunk by nobles
> whatever the hour we visited.

In 1773, James Boswell and Dr Samuel Johnson visited MacLaine of Lochbuie, on Mull. Boswell describes a meal of plain food, but with drink aplenty:

> Our supper was indeed but a poor one. I think a sort of stewed mutton was the principal dish. I was afterwards told that he had no spit, and but one pot, in which everything is stewed … He had admirable port. Sir Allan and he and I drank each a bottle of it. Then we drank a bowl of punch …

By the latter half of the eighteenth century a fledgling tourist industry was establishing itself in the Highlands, and some households had begun to equip themselves to cater for the new visitors. In 1803, near Loch Etive, a landlady provided Dorothy

Wordsworth, and her brother William, with 'an excellent supper – fresh salmon, a fowl, gooseberries and cream and potatoes … and the next morning boiled milk and bread'. At Loch Creran, though, the ferry house seemed too wretched to eat in. The women there:

> … had just taken from the fire a great pan full of potatoes, which they mixed up with milk, all helping themselves out of the same vessel and the little children put in their dirty hands to dig out of the mess at their pleasure.

The diet of many ordinary folk at this time was simple but healthy. In 1793, stopping in Glen Croe on the way from Loch Lomond to Inveraray, Thomas Garnett reported that the people there ate '… milk, oatmeal and potatoes, with fish caught in the stream or herrings from Loch Long or Loch Fyne, and now and then a little mutton …'

But by the late 1850s, when the majority of the stories here were collected, many of the people in the West Highlands and Islands who enjoyed these tales as part of their popular entertainment had endured a decade of relative destitution. Battered by the repeated failure of the potato crop, tithed by an oppressive feudal system struggling through its last days, they had been brought close to poverty.

In the stories, though, abundance and hospitality prevail, sometimes in dramatic ways. The feast at Ballymeanoch, and the MacVicar and MacKellar wedding celebrations, both have unexpected outcomes, while Tall Inary's obligations to her guests drive her to the edge of despair.

John Dewar, who worked with J.F. Campbell collecting Argyll stories in the 1850s, heard the story of Bloinigein from his mother. The name means 'Fatty' in Gaelic, and 'Chubbykins' is my own interpretation.

'The Brown Bear of the Green Glen' is one of the great, old, rambling quest stories, and food and drink are at its heart – a bottle of whisky, a loaf of bread and a cheese. It was taken down from the telling of John MacDonald – 'travelling tinker' – who also told the wonderful 'Tale of the Soldier', which is in 'Tellers of Tales'. In this story Erin is, of course, Ireland.

The meaning of Killinochonoch given in the following story is a folk etymology. The actual meaning is uncertain.

~ The Ballymeanoch Feast ~

At Ballymeanoch in Kilmartin Glen, clearly visible to the traveller on the A816, six massive slabs of stone stand in a field. They are said to have been put in place around 4,000 years ago, with the purpose of predicting the midwinter positions in the sky of both the sun and the moon. Nearby is a seventh stone, which was broken and fell over in 1881. There's a hole through it, and the stone has been associated with courting rituals that took place in earlier days. In those same times lived the Lady of Ballymeanoch, a shrewish woman who was always feuding with her neighbours. One day she surprised her enemies by inviting them all to a banquet of reconciliation.

The banquet was held in a barn. The guests were seated round a single table, in such a way that each neighbour was placed next to one of the woman's close friends or relatives. A massive haggis was brought in and placed before the lady, who drew her dirk and commanded, 'Let my friends do as I do.' As she stabbed the haggis, each of her followers brought out his or her own dirk, and stabbed their neighbour. Forty people died, but one man managed to escape. He ran out of the barn and off through the fields crying in woe, 'Och-on-och, och-on-och!' Even today, the place where he fell is called Killinochonoch, the Burial Place of Och-on-och.

~ The MacVicar and MacKellar Wedding ~

The MacVicars of Dail-chruinneachd – the Meadow of the Gathering – in Glen Aray, wanted their son to marry the daughter of the MacKellars of Mam in Glen Shira, which was over the moors to the east. The girl was also being courted by Young MacKellar of Kilblaan, but this meant nothing to the MacVicars.

One night a party which included MacVicar and his son called on the MacKellars to sound out the girl's parents. When they reached Mam the house was silent, as the inhabitants were already in bed. MacVicar knocked at the door, and MacKellar called out, 'Who's there?'

'A friend,' replied MacVicar. 'Let us in.'

'If you are friends, I'll let you in,' said MacKellar. He got up and unbarred the door, and MacVicar and his crew entered. MacKellar's wife rose and lit a lamp. One of MacVicar's party produced a bottle of whisky, and asked if she had a quaich, a double-handled drinking bowl. The quaich was produced and filled, and the man offered it to MacKellar's wife, telling her, 'Drink to us.'

'Before I drink, tell me what is it that I'm drinking to?'

'We're building a house in Dail-chruinneachd,' said MacVicar. 'We're putting in the roof beam couples, but we only have one and we need two. Ours is made of oak, and we've heard that you have one that will match it; so we've come to see whether you'll give it to us.'

MacKellar didn't understand what MacVicar was driving at. He thought he was talking about building a roof, but in fact he was suggesting a marriage between their children. 'I have a half-couple,' said MacKellar, 'but it's made of ash. Ash and oak don't go so well together, for oak is much the longer-lasting of the two.'

'Ash lasts a good while,' said MacVicar, 'if you take care of it and keep it dry. But I suspect that you haven't looked closely at your half-couple, and that in fact it's made of oak, like ours.'

The man with the bottle asked MacKellar's wife where their daughter was.

'Euphemia has gone to bed. What do you want to say to her?'

'I want to give her a drink, as the quaich's going round. Where is she?'

The woman pointed to the door of the room. MacVicar's son said that it would be best if the girl got up, so they could get a look at her. So Effie got up and put on her clothes, and the man with the bottle and Young MacVicar took the lamp and went into the room. The man with the bottle gave the quaich of whisky to Effie and talked to her for a while in a low voice, then left her and Young MacVicar alone. For a good while they were whispering together.

At last Young MacVicar and Effie came out of the room and joined the rest of the company. 'Well, you're up,' said Effie's mother. The girl replied that she had heard the sounds of merriment, and wanted to join in the fun.

The man with the bottle said, 'We are putting another couple in the roof of the house, and Young MacVicar will be one side of it. How would it be, goodman and goodwife, if your daughter Effie were to be the other?'

The old couple were silent. The man with the bottle asked again if MacKellar would give his daughter to be married.

'There she is,' said MacKellar, 'ask her yourself.'

'If my parents are agreeable,' said Effie, 'I would be very agreeable indeed.' Her mother and her father both told her that they wouldn't come between them, if the young couple were happy with the match.

A day was fixed for the agreement, the start of the marriage process, which was to be held on the top of the moor between Mam and Dail-chruinneachd, in the place where people left their peats to dry after they had been cut.

The day for the agreement came, and the two parties, together with their friends, arrived on the tops among the peats, each bringing a horse carrying creels loaded with food and whisky. The whisky was sent round and the terms of the agreement pronounced at length, until everyone was satisfied. At last the two young people were brought before the company, and asked if they were willing to marry. They said that they were, and joined hands, and so the agreement was made.

A date was fixed for the marriage and everyone present at the agreement was invited. Then a cloth was spread out and there was a great feast. After the food was all gone, the whisky kept flowing in a never-ending stream. The men drank and the women sang, and after a while most of the men were drunk. One of them fell into a peat bog and had to be hauled out. He was left on the grass to dry out, and many others joined him, spending the night in his company because they were incapable of finding their way back home.

The day of the wedding came and there were many guests. A hundred spoons were lifted at supper. After the meal there was music, merriment and drinking. The young couple were married, and they were sent to bed in a little room with only a wooden partition between them and the chamber where the festivities were still going on.

Angus MacKellar of Kilblaan, who had been courting Effie before young MacVicar came on the scene, was sitting opposite MacKellar of Mam. He felt he had been cheated of a wife, but spoke in a placatory way to the girl's father. 'She's a sensible woman, and he's a decent enough man.'

'I'll drink to your health for those words,' said MacKellar of Mam, stretching out his hand to Angus, but when Angus put out his own hand MacKellar of Mam made a fist and stuck out his first finger, in a gesture that insultingly parodied a man's privates. Angus grabbed hold of the finger, took a knife from his pocket, and cut it off.

A fierce fight started. Some took Angus' side, others that of MacKellar of Mam. The wooden partition was knocked down, and the young couple had to rise and get dressed. There was a big man in the room who didn't join in the fight, but just sat, watching. When the brawlers started to tire he began to separate them, and to reason with them, until each man had left, and made his way back to his own home.

Angus MacKellar was forced to flee, and was never seen again in those parts.

~ Tall Inary and Her Long Night ~

There was a farmer's wife who lived in the west of Mull, near Burg hill, which was known to be a *sìthean*, a fairy dwelling. People called the woman Tall Inary. Inary often stayed up after her husband and the rest of the family had gone to bed, working wool to make cloth for the household. She took on the whole business, from teasing to weaving, while the fulling water – the accumulated contents of the chamber pot, which was used to shrink the cloth – warmed in a pan over the fire. Late one evening she was so exhausted, she couldn't stop herself crying out, 'If only I could get help! I don't care where it's from – land or sea or air, near or far – somebody please come and help me make this cloth.'

There was a rap at the door. A voice called from out of the night, in a language Inary had never heard before, but which she could somehow understand. 'Tall Inary, good housewife, open the door and I'll help you until I can help no more.'

The farmer's wife opened the door to an odd-looking woman dressed in green. The woman walked past without looking at Inary, sat down at the spinning wheel, and began to spin. As soon as she sat, there was an even louder knocking, and another voice called out, 'Tall Inary, good housewife, open the door and I'll help you until I can help no more.' Inary let in another strange, green-clad woman, who glided past her and started to card the wool. Soon the house was full of fairy people, men and women, all working away at teasing, carding, spinning and weaving, and the noise in the room grew louder and louder with the whirring, the rasping, the clicking and the clunking, and the sound of the fulling water bubbling and hissing over the fire.

Inary tried to quell the hubbub, and she began to bring food for the workers, to fulfil her duties as a hostess. Soon all the bread and butter, the cheese and meat, were gone, and her cupboard was bare. She went to the kist for oatmeal, and began to bake bannocks, which the fairy people gobbled up. Inary was even more exhausted than she had been at the start of the whole business, when she had first called for help. Gobbets of sweat fell from her forehead and plopped on the floor.

By midnight, Inary was in despair. She went to rouse her husband, but he was so sound asleep she might as well have tried to wake a log of wood. Then she remembered an old man who lived in the township, and who knew about mysterious things. Inary slipped out of the farmhouse and went through the fields until she came to the old man's cottage. He listened to her story of the relentless woollen workers, and the husband who couldn't be woken, and then he gave his verdict: 'You shouldn't have asked for help in the way that you did. From now on, be careful what you wish for, or your wishes might be fulfilled by helpers you can't cope with. Your guests have moved in now, and you won't persuade them to leave with sweet words. As for your husband, he's under a spell, and he won't be wakened until the unwelcome visitors are out of the house, and you've sprinkled him with some of the fulling water.'

Inary asked the wise man how she could get rid of the fairies. He told her to stand on the hillock outside the farm, and to shout 'Burg hill is on fire!' three times. They would come to see what was happening. When they were all outside, Inary was to slip back in the house, bolt the door, and make sure that everything in there was upside down, back to front, or topsy turvy.

Inary thanked the old man, and went back over the fields. She stood on the mound outside the farm and shouted, 'Burg hill is on fire! Burg hill is on fire! Burg hill is on fire!' Even before she had finished shouting, the people in green had begun to leave the house, jamming themselves in the door and crushing each other underfoot, trying to find out what was happening to their home. In their panic they called after the things that were most dear to them:

My wife and little ones
My cheese and butter-keg
My sons and daughters
My big meal chests
My comb and wool-cards
My distaff and spinning wheel
My cattle and horses
My plough and anvil
Burg hill is on fire!
If Burg hill is on fire
Everything will be lost

When the last of the fairies was outside, Inary slipped back into the house and bolted the door. She took the band off the spinning wheel, and twisted the distaff the wrong way. She put the wool cards with their handles together, turned the loom upside down, and took the pot that held the fulling water away from the fire.

She had hardly finished when there was a knocking at the door.

'Tall Inary, let us in.'

'I can't. I'm up to my elbows in dough.'

'Spinning wheel, open the door.'

'How can I, when my band is off?'

'Distaff, throw back the bolt.'

'I would if I could, but I'm twisted the wrong way.'

'Wool cards, there's work to do.'

'We'd let you in, but our handles are put together and we can't move.'

'Loom, help us finish our task.'

'If only I were able, but I'm upside down.'

'Fulling water, rich and strong, you're our last hope.'

'I'm away from the fire. I have no strength left in me.'

The voices outside were becoming irritable. There was one last hope for them. Inary hadn't noticed that a little bannock had been left cooking away after all the others had been eaten; but the fairies knew it was there.

'Little bannock, sweet bannock, we need to get in and finish our work.'

The bannock hopped off the griddle and ran towards the door, but Inary grabbed him and threw him to the ground, where he broke in a dozen pieces.

The fairy people were furious. They had been tricked twice over. They went round the side of the house and gathered outside the bedroom window, where Inary's husband was asleep, and they screamed to be let in. Inary watched as her husband's head began to change shape, taking on all kinds of strange forms, until she became afraid that it would explode. Then she remembered what the old man had told her. She fetched the fulling water and threw it over him, not just a sprinkle, but the whole pot full.

Inary's husband woke. He got up, went to the door, and opened it. Outside there was darkness and silence.

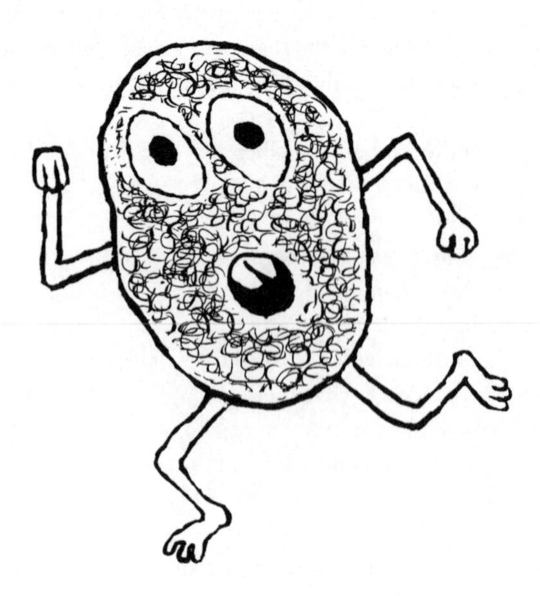

~ Chubbykins ~

There was a widow who had a son called Chubbykins. Together they built a house halfway up a hill. They thought they would be happy there forever, but it wasn't long before the widow died, and Chubbykins was left to fend for himself.

One day Chubbykins ventured out of the house. He looked up the hill and down the hill, and he saw the Old Hag coming towards him. She was a big blob of a thing. She only had one tooth in her mouth, and it was so long she was using it as a staff to help her up the hill. Chubbykins didn't like the look of her one bit. He zipped back inside and hid in a cupboard.

The Old Hag came into the kitchen. Chubbykins could hear the tooth tap tapping on the flags as she rootled around. 'Are you in, Chubbykins?' called the Old Hag. Chubbykins said nothing, though he was afraid the sound of his chattering teeth would give him away. 'If you're in, I've got some bread and cheese for you,' said the Hag.

Chubbykins came out of the cupboard. He was starving. He hadn't had a bite since his mother passed away. The Old Hag grabbed him, and popped him in a sack. She swung the sack over her shoulder and set off down the road. As she was going through a wood, she passed a bush that was weighed down with big, fat blackberries. The Old Hag loved blackberries. She put down the sack and, while she was stuffing the berries into her mouth, Chubbykins crept out of the sack, filled it up with stones, and tiptoed back home.

When the Old Hag put the sack back on her shoulder, it seemed heavier than before. 'Hey Chubbykins,' she said cheerily, 'I think you've put on weight.' By the time the Old Hag got back home, her daughter had the cauldron bubbling over the fire.

'Chubbykins is nice and fat,' said the Hag. 'We'll eat well tonight.' She tipped the stones out of the sack into the cauldron, the bottom of the cauldron fell out, and the scalding water went all over the feet of the Old Hag and her daughter. They danced around the kitchen like demons at a disco. 'Spit and sawdust!' screeched the Hag. 'Chubbykins will pay for this! It won't happen again!'

When the Old Hag's feet had healed, she set off once more to get Chubbykins. It just happened that, as the Hag was coming up the hill, Chubbykins had plucked up the courage to venture out of the house. He looked up and looked down and saw the Old Hag coming towards him, with her tooth clack clacking in front of her on the stones, so he bolted inside and hid in the attic. The Hag came into the kitchen. She went up to the hearth and, with a mighty puff, filled the whole house with glowing embers.

'Hey,' shouted Chubbykins, 'what are you up to? You'll burn the place down.'

'Are you there, Chubbykins?'

'Yes, I am.'

'Come on down so I can get a look at you.'

'I certainly won't, not after last time.'

'I was so fond of your poor, dear mother, and I'm even fonder of you. You're the sweetest thing I've ever set eyes on. Come on down, my little morsel.'

'I think you're flattering me.'

'Of course I'm not. Come on down and make an old woman happy.'

Chubbykins came down. The Old Hag grabbed him, threw him in her sack, and took him home. Her daughter already had the water heating, so the Hag popped Chubbykins in the cauldron and slammed on the lid. Then she went out into the forest to get more firewood, and left the daughter to keep an eye on things.

'This water is wonderfully warm,' called Chubbykins from inside the cauldron.

'Can I get in too?' asked the Old Hag's daughter.

'I'm afraid there's only room for one, and it's so deliciously cosy I just want to stay here all day.'

The Hag's daughter waited a while but, when she couldn't stand it any longer, she lifted the lid of the cauldron. 'Get out of there,' she ordered. 'My mother said before she went to get firewood that I was to get a turn as well.'

Chubbykins hopped out of the cauldron. 'You can't have long. Get right down in there, and I'll put the lid on so you can see how delightful it is.'

The Hag's daughter climbed into the cauldron. Chubbykins put the lid on nice and tight. He built the fire up to a good roar, and the girl in the cauldron started to scream to be let out. Chubbykins shouted back that she hadn't yet had the turn her mother had promised.

When the screams from inside the pot had ceased and the only sound was the bubbling of water, Chubbykins peeped out through the little hen hole in the cottage door and saw the Old Hag approaching, with her arms full of sticks. He hid in a dark corner behind the milk churn and watched her build up the fire. The Hag called to her daughter, and couldn't understand why there was no answer. But she understood well enough when, ready for her meal, she lifted the lid of the cauldron and there, inside, was the girl, boiled to a tender turn. The Hag ranted and raged. 'That greasy little maggot Chubbykins! He'll pay for this!' She picked up a pail, went to the milk churn and poured out a few dregs. As she was bending over, Chubbykins grabbed a mallet, and knocked out her brains. On his way home, he made up a song. This is how it went:

Nothing much for me back there
A blob of butter on a glowing ember
A drop of milk in a wicker basket
A drink of water from a bowl with no bottom
A couple of crumbs of invisible bread
And so I went home

– The Brown Bear of the Green Glen –

There was once a King of Erin, a good king, who had three sons. The two oldest were a couple of chancers and the youngest, John, was considered to be a bit of a simpleton.

The old king was ailing badly; he was blind and his legs weren't much use to him. The two oldest sons said that they would travel over the sea and to the end of the world to bring back three bottles of the water of the Green Isle, which was famous for its healing powers. After they left, John thought he fancied going too, so he set off on a lame white horse. That evening he caught up with his brothers, who were partying in a nearby town. 'Hop it,' they told him. 'Push off back to the castle.'

'Not to worry,' said John. 'Sorry to bother you, I'll go on by myself.'

John kept going until he came to a great tangle of a wood. 'Ooh,' he said, 'this isn't a place to be travelling alone.' It was growing dark, so John found a stout tree, tied up the horse and climbed high into the branches. As he sat there he noticed a dim red light in the distance, and it was coming towards him. The light got closer and John saw that it was a glowing coal, and it was in the mouth of a bear.

The bear reached the bottom of the tree. 'Come on down, son of the King of Erin,' it called up.

'I certainly will not,' John called back down. 'I reckon I'm a lot safer where I am.'

'If you won't come down, I'll have to come up,' said the bear.

'You must think I'm stupid,' said John. 'How could a great shaggy lump like you get up a tree?'

'Watch me,' said the bear, and began to climb.

'You aren't joking,' said John. 'All right, I'll come down, so long as you keep your distance.' So John came down the tree, and he and the bear started to chat. The bear asked whether he was hungry.

'I could manage a bite,' said John.

The bear rampaged off into the darkness and returned with a roebuck between its jaws. 'How do you like your roebuck, raw or cooked?'

'I'm used to having my meat cooked,' said John; and that was how it was, he got it roasted.

'Lie down and I'll put my paws around you,' said the bear, 'and you'll be snug and safe until morning.' At first light, the bear whispered, 'Are you asleep, King of Erin's son?'

'Not really,' replied John.

'Time to be on your feet, then. You've got a long journey ahead, a couple of hundred miles. On the other hand, how good a rider are you?'

'There have been worse,' said John.

'Hop on my back, then.' John climbed up onto the bear, but with the first bound he landed back on the ground, on his backside. He climbed up again, and this time he clung on not just with his fingers but with his teeth.

At the end of the two hundred miles they reached a giant's house. 'Now John,' said the bear, 'you're going to have to spend the night here with the giant. He's a cantankerous character, but if you tell him that the Brown Bear of the Green Glen sent you, you'll get good board and lodging.'

When the giant saw John, he said, 'I've been expecting you for a long time. Your coming was foretold. If I haven't got the father, at least I've got the son of the King of Erin. I don't know whether to grind you into the ground with my foot, or puff you off into outer space.'

'I don't think you'll do either,' said John, 'since it was the Brown Bear of the Green Glen who sent me.'

'Ah, that's different,' said the giant. 'Come in, come in, and you'll be well looked after.' And it was true enough; John got more than his fill of food and drink in the giant's house.

To cut a long story short, John got another ride from the bear the following morning, and spent the night at a second giant's house under the same terms as the night before.

Next day, they arrived in the evening at the house of a third giant. 'I don't know this giant so well,' said the bear, 'but you won't be long in there before he starts to wrestle with you. If he gets the better of you, just say, "I wish my master, the Brown Bear of the Green Glen, were here."'

As soon as the giant clapped eyes on John he began to screech with delight. 'If I haven't got the father, at least I've got the son,' he squawked, and grabbed John in a vicious headlock. John and the giant went at it. They churned the rocks up into bog. Wherever the stone was hardest they sank up to their knees, and where it was softest they were up to their thighs. Wherever they put their feet, fresh springs gushed out of the earth. John was getting the worst of it. 'If my master the Brown Bear of the Green Glen was here,' he said to the giant, 'you wouldn't be doing so well.'

No sooner had John spoken than the trusty bear was at his side. When the giant saw the bear, he set John down. 'Why didn't you tell me before that he was your master, son of the King of Erin? Now I know exactly what has to be done.'

The giant ordered his shepherd to fetch the finest wether he had on the hill, and to throw its carcase down in front of the big door. 'Now John,' said the giant, 'an eagle will come and settle on the carcase. The eagle has a wart on her ear.' The giant gave John a sword. 'You must cut off the wart with this sword, without drawing a drop of blood.'

Sure enough, the eagle came down, and started to eat from the wether's flesh. John swung the sword, and cut off the wart, and there wasn't a drop of blood to be seen. Then the eagle spoke to John. 'Climb up between my wings, for I know just what to do next.' John climbed up between the eagle's wings, and they flew over glens and mountains and seas until they reached the end of the world and the Green Isle.

'Now John,' said the eagle, 'go to that well and fill up three bottles; and be quick about it, or the black dogs will be after us.' When John had filled up the three bottles, he noticed that there was a little house close by. He went in and, on a table in the first room, he found a bottle full of whisky. John poured a glass and drank – and good whisky it was – and when he looked again at the bottle it was as full as when he came in. 'I'll take that back with me, together with the three bottles of water,' he said to himself.

John went into a second room, where he found a loaf. When he cut a slice from it, the loaf became whole again in an instant. 'I'll take that as well,' he said. It was the same with the big cheese he found in the third room. And in the fourth room there was as pretty a little jewel of a woman as he'd ever seen. 'It would be a shame not to have a kiss, my sweet,' said John.

After a little while John went out and climbed back up on the eagle's back, and they returned to the house of the wrestling giant, who was throwing a party for his tenants. 'Well John,' said the giant boastfully, 'did you ever see a feast like this in the court of the King of Erin?'

'Pooh,' said John. 'It's nothing to what I have here. Look at this, and marvel.' He showed the bottle of whisky to the giant. The giant poured himself a dram and, as soon as he did, the bottle was full again, right to the top.

'I've got to have that,' said the giant. 'I'll give you two hundred pounds, together with a saddle and a bridle.'

'Done,' said John. 'But you must surrender it to the first sweetheart I ever had, if she happens to pass by this way.' The giant agreed to John's terms, and, to cut a long story short, John sold the loaf and the cheese to the other two giants, on condition that they give them up to his very first sweetheart, if she ever chanced to pass their way.

So John at last found himself back in the town where he had left his brothers. They were still partying. 'Come on lads, I've got the three bottles of water from the Green Isle. Let's get back to our father so we can make him better as soon as possible. I'll buy you both a decent suit of clothes, and you'll get a horse and a saddle and bridle each, into the bargain.'

And that's what happened; but when they were close to their father's house the two older brothers decided to kill John. They set upon him and, when they thought he was dead, they threw his body over a stone wall, took the three bottles, and went back home. John wasn't long at the back of the wall before he heard the sound of iron-rimmed wheels coming up the road. 'Whoever you are,' he shouted, 'please help me.' It was his father's smith, with a cart full of rusty old iron.

The smith looked behind the wall and saw John, so bruised and bloody he didn't recognise him. 'I need someone to help out in the forge,' said the smith. 'Maybe you'll do.' And he heaved John on to the back of the cart, among the rusty iron. The iron was so sharp it went into John's wounds and made them even worse, and the shock was so great that all his hair fell out. So John became scarred, and as bald as a goose egg.

And there, for a while, we leave him.

Not long after John left his first sweetheart, the prettiest little jewel, on the Green Isle, she grew pale and her waist began to thicken; and nine months later she gave birth to a baby boy. 'How did this happen?' she asked the hen-wife, the wise woman who had helped her give birth.

'Too late to worry about that now. Just take this little bird. When he sees your son's father, he'll hop on to his head, and you'll know who he is for sure.'

Everyone who lived on the Green Isle formed a long queue. One by one, they passed though the house, in the back door and out the front, but the bird didn't stir a feather. The girl said she would search to the ends of the earth for the father of her baby, wherever he might be. She came to the house of the first giant, and saw the bottle. 'Where did you get this bottle?' she asked.

'I got it from John, the son of the King of Erin.'

'Well, I would like it back.' The giant gave her back the bottle, and, to cut a long story short, as she went from giant's house to giant's house, she got back the loaf and the cheese as well. Then she came to the house of the King of Erin. Everyone who lived in Erin formed a long queue, and, one by one, they passed though the house, in the back door and out the front, but the bird didn't stir a feather. The girl asked if there was anyone else at all living in Erin who hadn't been there yet.

'There's my gillie,' said the smith. 'You wouldn't be interested in him. He's covered in scars and bald as a goose egg.'

'Bald or not, send him here.'

As soon as John arrived, the bird hopped on to his head. The girl threw her arms round him and kissed him. 'My baby's father,' she said.

The King of Erin spoke. 'John, I have an idea it was you who brought back the three bottles of water that have cured me.'

'Indeed it was.'

'Well, what do you think we should do to your two brothers?'

'Do to them what they tried to do to me.' And that's how it was.

There was a great wedding between John and the daughter of the King of the Green Isle. It lasted for seven years and seven days, and the last time I passed by, the fiddles were still playing and the feet were still flying.

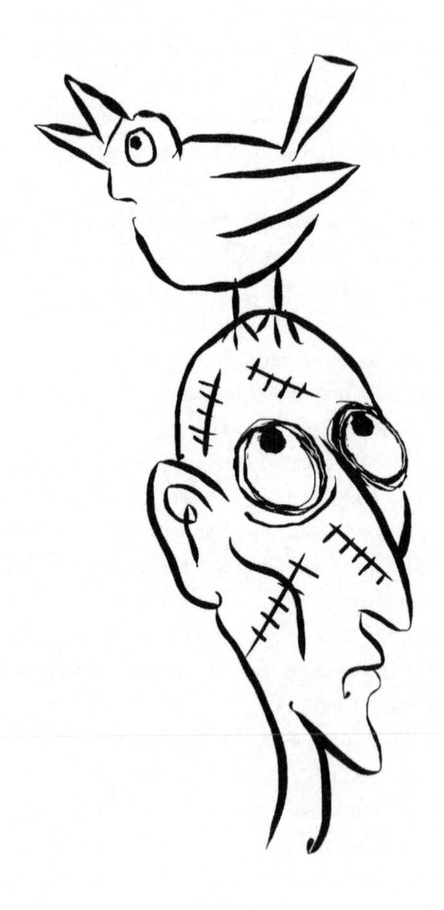

Guide to Gaelic Pronunciation

Below is a very simplified guide to the approximate pronunciation of words and phrases in the tales, plus any unusual personal names, listed in alphabetical order. Note that 'ch' sounds as in Scottish 'loch' (not as in 'chair); 'g' is hard, as in 'girl'; there is no exact English equivalent for 'ao'– the nearest is like 'cool' but said with unrounded lips, or (used here) *eu* as in French *neuve*. Underlines show stress, usually on the first syllable. Detailed phonetic guides to Scottish Gaelic are available online.

Boinne	*Bonn-yeh*
Cailleach Bheur	*Kye-ach Vee-ar*
ceilidh	*kay-lee*
Cuilionn	*Cooleen*
daoine sìth	*deun-yeh shee*
Diarmid	*Jee-armit*
Doideag	*Doy-chak*
dubh-brochan	*doo-brochan*
Fearachar	*Fer-achar*
Ghlaisrig Ileach	*Glas-rik Ee-luch*
Gormshuil Mhòr a Lochabar	*Gorrum-hool Vohr a Lochaber*
Grainne	*Gran-yeh*
Is mairg an losg mi an tiumpan dhuit	*Is mer-uk an losk mee an choompan gooch*

Ladhrag Thiristeach	*La-rak Heerisht-uch*
mise mi fhin	*meesh-eh mee heen*
Naoise	*Neu-sheh*
puirt	*poorsht*
sìthean	*shee-an*
Thig an nuas	*Heek a noo-as*
Thig là a'choin duibh fhathast	*Heek la a chon doo ha-ast*
Triùir a thig gun iarraidh – Gaol, Eud is Eagal	*Tree-oor a heek goon ee-a-ree – Geul, Ee-ud is Ekul*
Uisne	*Oosh-neh*
ursgeulan	*oor-skeal-an*

Select Bibliography

Adomnán of Iona, *Life of St Columba*, translated by Richard Sharpe (London, 1995)

Black, Ronald (ed.), *The Gaelic Otherworld: John Gregorson Campbell's Superstitions of the Highlands and Islands of Scotland and Witchcraft and Second Sight in the Highlands and Islands* (Edinburgh, 2005)

Black, Ronald (ed.), *To the Hebrides. Samuel Johnson's Journey to the Western Islands of Scotland and James Boswell's Journal of a Tour to the Hebrides* (Edinburgh, 2007)

Campbell, Ewan, *Saints and Sea Kings: The First Kingdom of the Scots* (Edinburgh, 1999)

Campbell, John Francis, *More West Highland Tales*, translated by J.G.Mackay, 2 vols (Edinburgh 1940–1960, reprinted Edinburgh, 1994)

Campbell, John Francis, *Popular Tales of the West Highlands*, 4 vols (1st edn Edinburgh 1860–62, reprinted Edinburgh, 1994)

Campbell, Lord Archibald, *Records of Argyll* (Edinburgh, 1885)

Carmichael, Alexander, *Deirdire and the Lay of the Children of Uisne* (Inverness, 1972)

Carmichael, Ian, *Lismore in Alba* (Perth, 1947)

Driscoll, Stephen, *Alba: The Gaelic Kingdom of Scotland* (Edinburgh, 2002)

Garnett, Thomas, *Observations on a Tour through the Highlands and part of the Western Isles of Scotland*, Vol.1 (London, 1800)

Grant, I.F., *Highland Folk Ways* (London, 1961)

Grant, K.W., *Myth, Tradition and Story from Western Argyll* (Oban, 1925)

MacArthur, E. Mairi (ed.), *Iona through Travellers' Eyes* (Iona, 1991)

MacArthur, E. Mairi, *Iona: The Living Memory of a Crofting Community* (2nd edn, Edinburgh, 2002)

MacCulloch, Donald B., *Romantic Lochaber* (Edinburgh & London, 1939)

Mackay, J.G. (ed.), *The Wizard's Gillie and Other Tales* (London, 1912)

Mackay, Margaret A., 'Here I am in another world: John Francis Campbell and Tiree' in *Scottish Studies*, No.32, 1993–98 (Edinburgh, 1998)

MacKechnie, Revd John (ed.), *The Dewar Manuscripts*, Vol.1, Scottish West Highland Folk Tales collected 1860–80 by John Dewar (Glasgow, 1963)

Maclean, Charles, *The Isle of Mull. Placenames, Meanings and Stories* (Dumfries, 1997)

MacLean, J.P., *History of the Island of Mull*, Vol.1 (Ohio, 1922)

Ó Baoill, Colm and Bateman, Meg, *The Harps' Cry. An Anthology of 17th Century Gaelic Poetry* (Edinburgh, 1994)

Owen, Olwyn, *The Sea Road: A Viking Voyage Through Scotland* (Edinburgh, 1999)

Rusticus, *The Royal Route* (Greenock, 1858)

Stewart, Revd Charles, 'Parish of Strachur and Stralachlan' in *The Statistical Account of Scotland* (Edinburgh, 1792)

Thomson, Derick S. (ed.), *The Companion to Gaelic Scotland* (Oxford, 1983)

Waifs & Strays of Celtic Tradition, Argyllshire Series, 5 vols (London, 1889–95). Series directed by Lord Archibald Campbell. Collectors and editors: the Revd J. MacDougall (Vols I & III); the Revd D. MacInnes (Vol. II); the Revd J.G. Campbell (Vols IV & V)

Webb, Sharon, *In the Footsteps of Kings* (Kilmartin, 2012)

Wordsworth, Dorothy, *Recollections of a Tour Made in Scotland A.D.1803* (Edinburgh, 1894)

Argyll has numerous excellent local museums, history trails and heritage centres; a comprehensive list can be browsed at www.exploreargyll.co.uk, a website set up by Argyll & the Isles Tourism Co-operative Ltd. Libraries and tourist offices in the area can also provide further information.

Some Argyll material from oral sources is included in *Tocher*, journal of the Department of Celtic and Scottish Studies at Edinburgh University and on the website www.tobarandualchais.co.uk. Also based in Edinburgh is a research project dedicated to the Argyll folklore collector Alexander Carmichael: www.carmichaelwatson.lib.ed.ac.uk.

About the Author

Bob Pegg is a storyteller, musician, songwriter and author, with a history of acclaimed performances, going back to his 1960s folk music partnership with Carole Pegg, the London Royal Festival Hall debut of his iconic folk rock band Mr Fox, and recordings for the Transatlantic label.

Since 1989 Bob has lived in the Scottish Highlands, and has worked as a storyteller right across Scotland, including the Northern and Western Isles, and as far away as Scandinavia and Iceland. He has also initiated many community projects – the latest a series of Story Maps for Highland museums. In 2014 Bob was commissioned to write and perform *Warrior Blues*, an hour-long retelling of Homer's *Odyssey* in story, song and music.

Bob's book *Highland Folk Tales* was published in 2012 by The History Press followed in 2013 by *The Little Book of Hogmanay,* an anthology of Scottish New Year customs.

Also by Bob Pegg

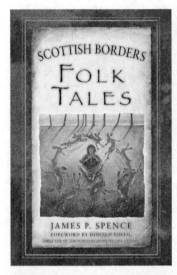

The Scottish Storytelling Centre is delighted to be associated with the *Folk Tales* series developed by The History Press. Its talented storytellers continue the Scottish tradition, revealing the regional riches of Scotland in these volumes. These include the different environments, languages and cultures encompassed in our big wee country. The Scottish Storytelling Centre provides a base and communications point for the national storytelling network, along with national networks for Traditional Music and Song and Traditions of Dance, all under the umbrella of TRACS (Traditional Arts and Culture Scotland). See www.scottishstorytellingcentre.co.uk for further information. The Traditional Arts community of Scotland is also delighted to be working with all the nations and regions of Great Britain and Ireland through the *Folk Tales* series.

Donald Smith
Director, Tracs
Traditional Arts and Culture Scotland

Printed in Great Britain
by Amazon